THE
CURSED

TWO ORIGINAL **CREEPSHOW**™ NOVELS

THE CURSED

BY ELLEY COOPER

Scholastic Inc.

ISBN 978-1-338-63124-1

1 2021

Printed in the U.S.A.   23

First printing 2021

Book design by Jessica Meltzer
Comic art by Brent Schoonover
Photos ©: Cover: AB Forces News Collection/Alamy
Images, Shutterstock.com.

For my parents, who were always willing
to check under my bed for monsters.

TABLE OF CONTENTS

CHAPTER 1

"Pardon me, ma'am," Randy said as he reached under the hen and retrieved a fresh-laid egg. He gently placed the egg in his basket and gave the butterscotch-colored bird a little pat. "Good girl, Anne Francis."

Randy had named all the hens after the stars of the movies he saw on the Saturdays when he got to go to town. Anne Francis played Altaira in *Forbidden Planet,* and Randy thought she was one of the most beautiful women he had ever seen. He called the arrogant black rooster, who sometimes charged up on him and pecked his legs, Godzilla. He knew that the rooster would stomp around and destroy cities, too, if he wasn't just a regular-size chicken. Two of the other hens, Zsa Zsa and Eva, were named after the glamorous Gabor sisters

3

who were always on the covers of the gossip magazines.

"Zsa Zsa's a good girl," Randy said, stroking the hen's soft white feathers. Daddy said it was foolish to name the chickens, that they were livestock, not pets. But Momma said she didn't see any harm in it, that Randy was still a child and children were supposed to have lively imaginations.

Daddy always said the same thing in response: "Randy is thirteen years old. I was already working in the mines when I was his age."

But Daddy didn't work in the mines anymore. Neither did any of the other men in the county. The mines had shut down two years ago, in 1954, and as a result, families that used to have enough food on the table and some extra money for Saturday movies and ice cream now had very little. It was the same all over the coal country of West Virginia, and boys like Randy who always figured they'd be miners once they left school now didn't know what they were going to be.

Randy moved on to Eva and wondered if she'd always known it would be her life's purpose to lay eggs, and if she liked her job. She was certainly good at it; she had an egg for Randy every single evening.

The truth was that while Randy missed the more-frequent trips to the movie house and the soda fountain since Daddy lost his job, he wasn't sad that his future wasn't all planned out for him anymore. He had never wanted to be a miner, never wanted to make his living doing back breaking labor in a dark, dangerous hole in the ground. He didn't want to live with the constant cough his daddy had from the dark and the damp, didn't want his fingernails to be permanently stained black no matter how much he scrubbed them.

"What do you think I ought to do with myself?" Randy asked Eva. It was a rhetorical question, but one that Randy thought about a lot. He liked taking care of the farm animals, but based on how his parents were struggling, he didn't see a future in farming. Daddy had to take on odd jobs just to make ends meet.

That being said, Randy didn't know what he wanted to be. He was old enough to know he couldn't be a space explorer or a cowboy or a jungle adventurer, but still, there had to be something better than what he was doing now, helping his family barely eke out an existence on their little plot of land in a remote hollow surrounded by mountains.

Randy finished gathering the eggs from the other chickens named after movie stars, then scattered cracked corn on the ground. "There you go, ladies and gentleman," he said. The chickens pecked at the corn, making satisfied little chortling noises.

Randy made his way past the barn, where Maybelle the cow (Randy's momma had named her) was chewing her cud, and up to their little unpainted wooden house.

Rufus, their black-and-tan hound, was on the porch, gnawing on a bone from the ham hock that had gone into tonight's pot of soup beans.

"How many eggs?" Momma said when Randy came into the house. She was washing the supper dishes at the sink. Her chestnut-brown hair was coming loose from the bun she always wore it in. Momma was a pretty woman, but ever since the mines closed, she looked tired.

"Eighteen," he said, setting the basket down on the kitchen table.

"Not bad," she said. "Some to eat and some to sell."

"Yes'm," Randy said, putting the clean dishes she had just dried into the cabinet.

"You got lessons tonight?" Momma asked. She always called homework *lessons*. She and Daddy both talked more country and old-fashioned than Randy did.

"I've got a little homework," Randy said.

Momma nodded. "Best get to it, then. I'll finish up here."

Because their house had only two small bedrooms, Randy shared his room with his five-year-old sister, Cindy. Momma had sewn a privacy curtain and hung it in the middle of the room so it was "just like you each have a room of your own." It wasn't really. But Cindy had an earlier bedtime than Randy and was a sound sleeper, so he could sit on his side of the room and do his homework or even listen to his transistor radio softly while she snoozed away.

Randy tried to pay attention to his math homework, but numbers never held his interest. He liked stories and excitement. Sometimes there were what the teacher called "story problems" in math, but the stories were boring, about how much of something somebody had or how fast a train was going. Instead of thinking about the train in the math problem, Randy fantasized about jumping on a high-speed locomotive and riding it all the way to Huntington or maybe even Cincinnati.

His fantasy was interrupted by a soft rapping on his window. "Shh," he hissed, afraid that the noise would wake Cindy.

He looked through the window. Bill, his best friend, who lived in the house across the road, pressed his face against the glass. Bill stretched out his mouth with his fingers and stuck out his tongue. "I'm the boogeyman come to get you!" he said, laughing.

Randy rolled his eyes and pushed up the window. "You're the sorriest excuse for a boogeyman I ever did see," he said. "Now, don't make too much racket. Cindy's asleep."

Bill climbed in through the window and took a seat on Randy's bed. Like Randy, Bill was clean but poor-looking. He had patches on the knees of his britches, and his sneakers were falling apart at the seams. But just about everybody Randy and Bill knew looked like this. Being poor wasn't as big a deal when everybody else was poor, too.

"You could use the door to come in, you know," Randy said, sitting down next to Bill.

"Yeah, but if I did your momma would know I was here, and she might tell my momma that I'm here. And strictly speaking, I ain't supposed to be here." He grinned, showing the gap between his two front teeth.

"And where are you supposed to be at?" Randy asked.

"Home in bed without supper," Bill said. "On account of that stunt I pulled in school. Say, you ain't got any leftover corn bread, do you?"

"We might. Sit tight. I'll be right back." Randy went into the kitchen. A few slices' worth of corn bread were in the cast-iron skillet sitting on the back of the stove. He cut off a hunk and got a glass of milk from the refrigerator, the appliance that Momma and Daddy still called "the icebox." Momma and Daddy were sitting on the couch listening to the radio. Daddy's job loss had killed any chance Randy's family had of owning a television any time soon.

"Growing boy, huh?" Momma said, nodding toward the snack Randy was holding.

"Yes, ma'am," he said, hightailing it to his room. He hadn't lied, exactly. He just hadn't said who the growing boy in question was.

"Thanks, buddy," Bill said, snatching the corn bread and the glass. "It don't hardly seem right, starving a feller half to death just cause he's a little high-spirited."

Randy smiled. "And leaving a cow pie in the seat of the teacher's desk—that was being high-spirited?"

Bill grinned. "It was."

"And so was beating up Carl Pruitt for telling on you?"

Bill nodded, his mouth full of corn bread. After he swallowed, he said, "That kid had it coming. There's something I don't trust about him. Between you and me, I think he's a communist."

Randy held back the urge to roll his eyes. This was not an unusual statement from Bill. He thought everybody he disliked was a communist. "Carl Pruitt? Really?" Randy said.

Bill nodded again. "They're everywhere, you know."

Randy had heard a lot in school about Russia and how bad communism was and how there were Americans who were members of the Communist Party trying to infiltrate normal American towns. Still, Randy wasn't as convinced as Bill that the regular people they met were communists in disguise. Why would anybody want to infiltrate a place as small and insignificant as Green Mountain, West Virginia?

"So I was thinking we might go camping on Saturday night," Bill said.

9

This was one of the reasons Bill was Randy's best friend even if they didn't always agree on everything. Bill could always think of fun things for them to do. "Camping, huh?" Randy said.

"Sure, my brother said we could use his pup tent. We've got a roll of baloney and some crackers at our house, so I could bring some of them. And maybe you could get your momma to boil some eggs and fix us a jug of fresh milk. We could stay up late as we want and tell ghost stories, and in the morning maybe we could walk over to Hatcher's Pond and go fishing."

It might not be an adventure like the ones he'd seen on the movie screen, but it was better than staying home and feeding the chickens. "Let's do it," Randy said. "If my folks say it's all right."

"They will," Bill said. "Your folks is way less mean than mine. Speaking of that, I'd better get home and in bed before I get caught, or they won't let me out to do nothing."

Bill was halfway out the window when Cindy, from the other side of the room, called, "Good night, Bill."

"Good night, Cindy," Bill said. "Sorry I woke you up sneaking in like I did."

"It's okay," Cindy said. "I won't tell on you. I ain't no communist."

CHAPTER 2

Daddy was sitting in the living room reading the newspaper. "Y'all gonna do any hunting while you're up there? Lots of rabbit this time of year."

Randy was rolling up a blanket and a pillow. It was the best he could do since he didn't have a sleeping bag. "No, sir, but we might do some fishing in the morning."

Daddy nodded and turned his attention back to the paper. "Try to catch us something good, then."

Momma came into the living room carrying a paper grocery bag. "All right, I fixed you three boiled eggs apiece and a jug of milk to share. There's also four cold biscuits with jelly."

"Thank you, Momma." The biscuits and jelly were an unexpected bonus. It would be nice to have something sweet.

Momma's brow wrinkled a little. "Now, you boys be careful in them woods. There's all kinds of wild animals there, and I worry about you'uns being up there by yourselves—"

Daddy looked up from his paper. "He's thirteen years old, Alma."

Momma smiled and shook her head. "I know, I know. And you was working in the mines when you was thirteen."

There was a pounding on the door that could only be Bill.

Randy ran to open it and found his friend, loaded down with camping gear. "Hey. You ready?" he asked. Randy could tell Bill was buzzing with excitement.

"Be careful, and have fun," Momma said.

The boys headed off in the direction of the woods while Bill recited the food items he was carrying. "I've got a half a pound of baloney, a full sleeve of saltine crackers, a can of pork 'n' beans, and four big dill pickles."

Randy listed the contents of the sack Momma had packed for them.

"Shoot," Bill said, grinning. "We're gonna have us a big old picnic, ain't we?"

"Yep." It was a beautiful day, the temperature warm but not hot, the sunlight bright but not blinding. Randy felt good walking into the woods with his best friend, walking toward adventure and away from chores and schoolwork. They hadn't even set up camp yet, and he was already having fun.

Once they were in the woods, they had to watch their step. It was an uphill walk, and the ground was treacherous with rocks and roots and twisting vines. It was pretty, though. Randy liked the way the sunlight shone through the trees, liked the sounds of the birds and the squirrels chirping and chittering. He liked how, in some places, the moss formed a soft green carpet under his feet.

"Snake," Bill whispered.

"Where at?" Randy whispered back.

"Over yonder," Bill said, pointing.

On a big, flat rock, a long black snake was stretched out, letting a sunbeam shine on him.

"Aw, that's just a black snake," Randy said. "He don't mean no harm unless you're a mouse or a rat. He's just getting a suntan, that's all."

Bill laughed. "How can a snake get a suntan?"

After a few more minutes of walking, they came to a clearing where the ground was surprisingly level. "You reckon this is our spot?" Bill asked.

"Looks like it to me," Randy said.

They set up the pup tent together, then gathered wood to start a campfire. Once the fire was going, Bill took out the pork 'n' beans, a can opener, and a small pan. They cooked the beans over the open fire, taking turns holding the pan just above the flame, until they got bored with the process and ate the beans cold out of the pan. Bill had neglected to bring spoons, so they tilted the pan up to their mouths and slurped. After that, they ate some baloney and crackers and a boiled egg and two dill pickles each, then passed the milk jug back and forth.

Randy patted his belly. "I'm full as a tick."

"Me too," Bill said. "Why don't we save the biscuits and jelly for after it gets dark, when we're telling ghost stories?"

"Good idea," Randy said. It felt good to be full. Since his daddy had lost his job, there had been nights when he'd gone to bed still hungry. Not because there'd been no food—Momma always managed to put something on the table—but because there hadn't been enough to sate his appetite. Like Momma said, he was a growing boy.

When darkness came upon them, it was as if a giant pair of hands had dropped a big black blanket over them. If it weren't for the flashlight Randy had packed and the campfire they had built, they wouldn't have been able to see their hands in front of them.

"Now it's time for spooky stories," Bill said.

Randy told a story his granny used to tell him about a ghost who haunted an old woman and kept telling her "I want my big toe!" It was a ghost story, but it was more funny than scary. Bill told a story about Old

Rawhide and Bloody Bones, who killed and ate children.

"My daddy always told me about Old Rawhide and Bloody Bones," Randy said. "He said he came to get little boys who wouldn't go to bed when they was supposed to."

"Mine told me the same thing!" Bill said, laughing. "That's why grown-ups make up them stories—to scare you into doing what they want you to do. I never believed 'em, though."

"I did when I was little," Randy said. "I figure just about every other kid in West Virginia believed Old Rawhide and Bloody Bones was hiding under their bed at one time or another."

"Not me, though," Bill said.

"Not ever?" *Surely*, Randy thought, *there was one time during Bill's childhood when he had been afraid of a strangely moving shadow that turned out to be a tree branch outside.* There had to have been a time or two when he lay curled in a ball in bed because of the fear that something hiding underneath might grab his ankle.

"Nope," Bill said. "I ain't no chicken. I don't want to be like that weird kid in school, James, who's always going on about monsters and ghosts, saying they're real."

"He is kind of . . . different," Randy said. James had moved to Green Mountain from Cincinnati at the beginning of the school year. Maybe it was because he was a city kid who talked and dressed different from everybody else, but he was definitely having a hard time making friends. He always sat at lunch by himself reading *Famous Monsters of Filmland* magazine. Randy felt sorry for him. He seemed lonely.

"He's a chicken is what he is," Bill said. "Always scaring himself about things that ain't real. I figure a chicken's about the worst thing you can be, besides a communist."

"Hey, I like chickens," Randy said. "I spend time with them every day."

"That don't mean you want to be one," Bill said.

"No, that's true." Randy had to admit that calling somebody a chicken because they were cowardly made a lot of sense. Chickens were scared of everything— noises, falling leaves, their own reflections. But they had a right to be scared. Nearly every other living creature wanted to eat them.

"Hey, you reckon it's time to eat those biscuits and jelly?" Bill asked.

"Sure."

The boys ate their biscuits, watching the last embers of the campfire die down and wiping their hands on their trousers mostly because their mommas weren't there to tell them not to. Then they doused the fire with a pan of water from the nearby creek, kicked dirt over it, and stomped it down to make sure no embers were burning.

With only the beam from Randy's flashlight to guide them, they crawled into the pup tent and snuggled down into their nest of blankets. Randy could feel every root and rock on the ground beneath his back, but somehow the tent was still cozy, maybe because Bill was right there with him.

Randy had almost settled into sleep when he heard a rustling outside. Something brushed against the tent. "Did you hear that?"

"Yeah." Bill's voice was fuzzy with sleep. "It's probably just a possum. Or if we're unlucky, a skunk."

Randy hoped it wasn't a skunk. Rufus the hound dog had gotten sprayed by a skunk once, and Randy had had to give him a bath with tomato juice. It had helped a little, but he still stank.

Whatever was outside the tent pushed it harder, almost collapsing one side.

"Uh . . . that's something bigger than a possum," Randy said. His heart beat faster. There were coyotes in the woods and sometimes bears.

"You reckon we should crawl out of the tent?" Bill asked. His voice sounded like he was wide awake now.

"We'd better. That way we can run if we have to." They were sitting ducks in the pup tent. Well, lying-down ducks, which was even worse.

Randy crawled out of the tent, holding the flashlight in his shaking hand. He hoped the light might spook the bear or coyote and cause it to run away. Randy rose to his feet and pointed the flashlight in the direction of the noise.

Then he laughed.

"What?" Bill said, coming out of the tent. "What is it?"

"It's the funniest-looking bear I ever did see," Randy said, shining his flashlight beam on a brown-and-white cow.

Bill laughed, too. "That's one of them cows from Hatcher's pasture. They get loose and wander off to the woods all the time. And you was so scared!"

"You was scared, too," Randy said, nudging Bill's shoulder.

"Was not." Bill patted the cow on the rump. "Get on home, Bessie!"

The cow ambled off in the general direction of the pasture.

"How did you know her name was Bessie?" Randy asked.

"I call all cows Bessie," Bill said. "They just look like Bessies to me."

Once the cow crisis was averted, they secured the tent and crawled back inside. Tired from all the excitement, Randy fell deeply asleep.

Randy was awakened by a low humming sound. It reminded him of a nest of wasps, but the sound was deeper, more musical somehow. Then, just as he was getting awake enough to try to make sense of things, the tent was illuminated with an eerie green glow.

Bill stirred and opened his eyes. "What the Sam Hill—?"

"I don't know," Randy said. This fear was different than when he thought there was a wild animal outside the tent. He had seen wild animals, had been taught what to do if faced with one. But he had no idea what could be producing that light and sound. It was a deeper fear, a fear that seemed to live in the pit of his stomach, the unsettling feeling of being afraid without having any idea what it was you were afraid of.

"Which is better, in the tent or out of the tent?" Bill asked, his voice trembling.

"I don't know that, either," Randy said. He took a deep breath. "But I'd rather know what it is than not know. I'm going out there."

He held fast to the flashlight even though he didn't need it. The green glow was almost as bright as the light cast by an electric light bulb. The light grew brighter as he made his way out of the tent. His legs shook as he stood. The glow was so bright now that he had to shield his eyes. He turned, squinting, to look at where it glowed the brightest.

And then his mouth dropped open in shock.

"Randy, are you okay?" Bill was scrambling out of the tent. "What is it?"

Even if Randy could have found the words in his brain, he couldn't form them with his mouth. He could only mutely point.

The thing was floating, hovering just above them. It was huge, larger than a big man, though, whether it was male or female was not apparent. It appeared to be wearing a green hooded cloak over a green flowing robe, which rippled in the breeze. Its face was hard to see because of the hood, but its eyes were red and round, sending out beams like headlights. The green glow seemed to be emanating from its entire body, circling it like a halo.

Randy and Bill looked at each other as if to confirm they were really seeing what they thought they were seeing.

And then they screamed.

The thing, whatever it was, did not respond to them in any way, nor did it show any signs of moving closer.

Well, Randy wasn't going to give it the chance to decide to get closer. There was only one word he could reach in the terrified recesses of his brain, and he yelled it now: "Run!"

He ran across the clearing, abandoning their campsite. He heard Bill's rapid footfalls right behind him.

But he wasn't going to look to see if the thing was chasing them. That's how people in movies always got in trouble. They looked back to see where the monster was, and then they lost their footing and fell, which gave the monster time to catch up with them.

The monster. That's what it was, wasn't it? He and Bill had seen a monster.

Running in the dark was hard, but Randy had his flashlight, and the remnants of the green glow kept the woods from being pitch-dark. All the same, Randy reached for Bill's hand so they could make their way over the roots and rocks together. At least this time they were going downhill.

When they reached the pasture that was between their houses, they wordlessly went their separate ways, Bill to his house, Randy to his. They were still running, though. Randy felt like his heart was going to thud right out of his chest.

The house was dark. He rushed to the front door and was relieved to find it unlocked. He swung open the door but froze when it creaked and willed himself to slow down. He didn't want to wake anybody up because he didn't want to have to explain why he was home early from the camping trip or what he had seen. How could he explain it when he wasn't sure what it was himself?

Once inside, Randy tore off his shoes and carried them, tiptoeing to his room in his socks. Cindy was sleeping peacefully. He jumped into his bed, shoes in his arms, and pulled the covers over his head. *Deep breaths*, he told himself, but his breathing was shallow, like a scared rabbit's, and he couldn't stop shaking. *You're safe*, he told himself. *It didn't follow you. You're safe.*

Just to make sure, he poked his head out of the covers and peeked out the window, half expecting to see the weird, glowing face looking right at him. But it wasn't there. Everything outside seemed ordinary until Randy moved his gaze out toward the mountains. He was pretty sure there was a faint green glow among the trees.

CHAPTER 3

Randy's family always tried to have a big noon dinner on Sunday, but it had gotten harder since Daddy lost his job. Back when the mining money was good, Sunday dinner would be two kinds of meat and all kinds of vegetables—corn on the cob, tomatoes and cucumbers, cabbage, fried okra—plus biscuits and corn bread. Today the meal was less lavish: country ham biscuits and some green beans Momma had canned last summer.

It was good food, but Randy didn't have much of an appetite. He was too panicked and puzzled by what he'd seen the night before. He was desperate to talk to Bill, but he knew there was no use trying to talk to Bill on a Sunday. For Bill's family, church was an all-day affair. There was Sunday school, then church services followed by a big picnic, then singing until it was time for the evening services. Momma made Randy and his sister go to church a couple times a month, but they were nowhere near as devout as Bill's family.

"Hey, I've eaten more ham biscuits than Randy," Cindy said, gesturing toward her brother with a biscuit in hand. "I've had three and he ain't had but one."

"Randy, are you feeling all right?" Momma asked. "You didn't catch a chill out in the woods last night, did you?"

"No, ma'am, I'm not sick," Randy said. He wasn't eating because what he saw the night before was tearing him up inside. He needed to talk about it, needed to unburden himself of the secret. He was a pretty quiet kid, but when something bad happened, the only way he could feel better was to talk about it. *Okay*, he told himself. *Out with it.* "Something happened last night that . . . troubled me," he said.

"Did you and Bill get in a fight?" Cindy asked, grinning around a mouthful of ham biscuit. She seemed pretty entertained by the prospect.

"No, nothing like that," Randy said. "I guess you could say we saw something."

"Did you come across somebody's still?" Daddy asked, spearing a forkful of green beans. It was common knowledge that there were lots of moonshiners who set up their illegal whiskey-making contraptions in the hills. They didn't take kindly to strangers who discovered their whereabouts.

"No, nothing like that, neither," Randy said, pushing his plate away. How could he explain something that seemed so unexplainable? What were the chances that anybody would even believe him? But Momma always said, *The truth will set you free.* If he was going to deal with what had happened, he had to tell the truth. He took a deep breath, then willed himself to speak. "We was asleep in the tent, and this strange light woke me up. It was green like some of the lights they put up downtown at Christmastime, except it gave off more of a glow. It woke Bill up, too, and we went outside to see what it was." He paused. Momma and Daddy and Cindy were all staring at him like he was a stranger who had sat down at the table with them, but he had to keep talking. He had to finish the story. "And to tell the truth, I can't tell you what it was. It was shaped kind of like a person but bigger, and you couldn't see its shape or its face real good because it had on this cape with a big hood. But its eyes were big and round and glowed red." He looked again at his parents' and sister's faces. They were all wearing looks of shock and confusion. Cindy looked like she was trying to figure out if he was joking or not.

Finally, Momma gave a nervous little laugh. "Well, I reckon you boys got to telling spooky stories out there in the dark woods and got yourselves all worked up. You probably just seen a big hoot owl or something."

"Yeah," Daddy said, "sometimes critters you wouldn't think nothing of in the daytime look down-right frightful at night. One time when I was taking out the trash in the evening, a possum sprung out at me and scared the living daylights out of me. It was baring its teeth and hissing, and its eyes glowed just like you was saying."

But owls and possums were nothing like what Randy had been describing. "No, it wasn't like that," Randy said. "It was big and green and floating and it gave off this light—"

"Sometimes our minds can play tricks on us," Momma said. "Especially when you're out at night with your friend and you've stayed up way past your bedtime trying to scare each other. I bet y'all hardly got a wink of sleep last night. Maybe you should lie down for a nap once you're done eating."

"I am done, Momma. Can I be excused?"

Randy didn't want to nap, but he saw it was point-less to continue the conversation. The more he insisted that he knew what he had seen, the more likely his family was to think he was crazy. He lay across his bed with a composition book and a pencil. He closed his eyes for a moment, picturing the monster, and then started to draw. He wasn't a great artist, but by the time he was done, he had a reasonably good likeness of what he had seen. It made him feel a little better to have the image, even though he didn't need to look at a picture to remember what the monster looked like. How could you see something like that and ever forget it?

And if someone had never seen a monster, you couldn't possibly make them understand what it was like. The only person who could understand was some-one who had had the experience, too. First thing tomorrow, he needed to talk to Bill.

Randy woke up Monday morning feeling hopeful. Once he talked to Bill, things would be clearer, and he would feel less alone.

"You feeling better now that you've had a chance to rest?" Momma asked as she set his breakfast of biscuits and gravy in front of him.

"Yes, ma'am," Randy said, though, of course he hadn't felt bad in quite the way Momma meant.

"Sometimes you just need to see things clearer in the light of a new day," Daddy said. He was drinking coffee and looking at the newspaper's want ads. He had a pencil ready to circle any possible jobs, but he hadn't circled anything yet.

Randy glanced at the cuckoo clock above the

icebox. Bill was never late, but apparently there was a first time for everything. An image of Bill huddled under the covers flashed in Randy's mind, and he regretted not trying harder to check on his friend yesterday. What if Bill was still curled up in bed, shaking from what they had seen?

There was a loud banging on the screen door and Randy jumped. Bill let himself in.

"Hi, Bill!" Cindy said, her whole face lighting up.

"Hey, Cindy," Bill said. He had his school satchel slung over his shoulder and was wearing slightly nicer clothes than the ones he wore just to play in.

So not still shaking in bed. *Good*, Randy thought.

"You got time for a biscuit this morning?" Momma asked.

"Not to sit down and eat one, but I'll take one for the road," Bill said, grinning.

"Yeah, we'd better get going," Randy said, getting up from the table. He wasn't particularly eager to get to school, but he was dying to get Bill alone so they could talk.

Momma handed Bill a warm biscuit wrapped in a napkin, and he bit into it immediately. "Thank you, Miz Siler. Your biscuits is better than my momma's, but don't tell my momma I said that."

Momma smiled. "I wouldn't dream of it."

Randy grabbed his books and the boys headed out.

They always walked together to the head of the hollow to catch the school bus. Randy figured the ten-minute walk would be a good opportunity for them to talk about what they had seen on Saturday night.

Once they were on the gravel road that led out to the main road, Randy said, "You know, I've been thinking a lot about that thing we saw."

"Me too," Bill said, "and I think I've got it all figured out."

"Figured out how?" Randy asked. If Bill had any ideas, Randy certainly wanted to hear them.

"Well, I had it figured out as soon as I seen it, really," Bill said. "It was a hoax. Like 'The War of the Worlds.'"

A hoax? The knot in Randy's stomach sure didn't think it was a hoax, but he also didn't know what Bill was talking about. "What's 'The War of the Worlds'?"

"It was a radio show that came on when my daddy was a little boy," Bill said. "It sounded like a news broadcast and was all about how the Martians had come to Earth and was about to take over. Daddy said it had his Pa so convinced that he was loading his rifle, ready to fight off the Martians."

"So you think the thing we saw wasn't real?" The thought hadn't even crossed Randy's mind.

Bill laughed. "Oh, I knew right away it wasn't

29

real! Here's what I think. It was the Russians who put out the hoax."

Randy stifled the urge to roll his eyes. "Why would the Russians try to trick us thataway?" Randy asked. "Especially you and me. We're just kids. We're not important to them."

"I'm sure we're not the only people it appeared to," Bill said. "If the Russians scare enough people with that thing and make everyone think we're under attack, then everybody would be so scared of aliens that they won't notice the Russians taking over the country."

Randy shook his head. "It looked real." He could see the round, glowing eyes just as surely as if they were staring at him right now.

"Sure it did. I'm sure the Reds got some of their best people working on it to make sure it looks real."

Randy didn't have an explanation himself for the incident, but Bill's explanation felt awfully farfetched. "So you say you knew it was fake when you saw it?"

"I sure did." Bill's shoulders were slung back. He looked pleased with himself.

"Then why was you so scared?"

Bill's eyes flashed mad. "I wasn't scared. *You* was the one that was scared."

Randy laughed. He remembered the look on Bill's face, the wide eyes, the slack jaw. "We was both scared. We screamed, then we ran like scalded dogs."

"Yeah, well," Bill said as they approached the bus stop. "I was just pretending to be scared to throw the Russians off track. You're the one who was the big chicken."

As much as Randy liked the chickens at the farm, he didn't want to be one. "Come on, Bill, we both had our britches scared off. Either both of us is chickens, or neither one of us is!"

Bill tucked his hands into his armpits and flapped his arms like wings. "Bock, bock, bock!" He danced around Randy. "A yellow coward's what you are. A big . . . yellow . . . chicken!"

Before Randy could think of a comeback, something else big and yellow arrived. He climbed onto the school bus first and took his customary seat on the third row by the window. For the first time he could remember, Bill didn't come sit beside him.

CHAPTER 4

School was lonely without Bill. It would've been lonely if Bill wasn't there, but it was even lonelier because Bill was present but ignoring Randy. Usually in class, Bill was always whispering to him or passing notes until they would get in trouble and have to write *I will not talk in class* twenty times on the board. But today Bill's mouth was closed, and his eyes were fixed on the teacher.

Usually Randy and Bill sat together at lunch, which was comfortable because they brought the same kind of poor country-kid lunches: cold biscuits with cheese or ham if they were lucky or with nothing if they were not, and hard-boiled eggs courtesy of their chickens. The town kids with money bought the lunch at the cafeteria or brought peanut butter and jelly sandwiches on store-bought white bread and shiny red apples that almost didn't look real. They made fun of the country kids' cold biscuits and leftovers.

But today, instead of sitting in his usual spot and saving a place for Randy, Bill was sitting with a bunch of kids he knew from the 4-H Club. Randy knew if he tried to sit down at the table with them, nobody would stop him. But he also knew that Bill would ignore him, and he'd rather be ignored by Bill from a distance than close-up. He bought a carton of milk with the nickel his mother always gave him and sat down by himself at the end of a long table. The cafeteria was noisy, full of talk and laughter. It was hard to be in a loud place when you were alone. He ate his cold biscuit in four big bites, then washed it down with the milk. He was more than ready to flee the crowded cafeteria. Feeling lonely in a crowd was the worst kind of lonely.

Randy always went to the school library when he could because he liked quiet and reading and found the environment to be restful. Today, though, he thought the library might be helpful in another way. He wondered, *might there be a book with some information about the thing he saw? Had other people ever seen it, too?*

He went to the big wooden chest that housed the library's card catalog. He pulled out the drawer for books with subjects starting with *M* for *Monsters*.

Most of what he found wasn't very helpful. He

discovered cards for *Dracula* and *Frankenstein*, but it hadn't been either one of them he saw up on the mountain Saturday night. He flipped through a few more cards, then found one that piqued his interest. The book was titled *Meeting Monsters: On the Track of Unlikely Beasts and Unexplained Phenomenas.* Unexplained phenomenas . . . that's what he had experienced, wasn't it? Maybe this book could explain it to him. Remembering the book's place according to the Dewey Decimal System, he went into the stacks and pulled it right off the shelf.

"Interesting stuff," Miss Pitt the librarian said when he handed her the book at the checkout desk.

"Yes, ma'am," Randy said shyly. If he was being honest with himself, he'd have to say that another reason he liked the library was because the librarian was young and pretty. She had a headful of dark curls, and he liked the way her glasses made her look smart.

Randy really wanted to go home and read his book, but he knew he had to endure the rest of the school day. And there would be chores as soon as he got home— more obstacles to getting his unexplained phenomena explained.

During social studies class, the students were herded into the gym so they could watch a film about protecting themselves when the Russians dropped the atomic bomb. The film showed kids younger than Randy hiding under their desks at school or jumping off their bicycles and lying down on the side of the road when they heard the nuclear blast. There was even a scene of a family having a picnic, then hiding under the tablecloth and napkins when the bomb went off. Randy doubted this would be much help, but he was sure Bill was paying close attention and maybe even taking notes. He always said a nuclear attack by the Russians was not a matter of *if*, but *when*.

Randy thought back to his disappointing conversation with Bill this morning. Why was Bill determined to think the thing they saw was some kind of Russian hoax? If the Russians had the power to blow America to kingdom come any time they wanted to, what would be the point of making a spooky-looking creature just to scare a couple of kids in the middle of nowhere in West Virginia? Also, Randy wasn't convinced that even the Russians could make a creature that looked as convincingly real as the one they saw. Even in the movies, things didn't look that real. You could always see where the zipper went on the suit or the string the flying saucer was dangling from.

After a silent bus ride home, Randy stepped off the bus behind Bill. "Okay, Bill," Randy said. "We're the only kids that live in this holler, and we live right next door to each other. Are we gonna walk all the way home without saying a word to each other?"

"I'm not gonna say a word to you as long as you

keep talking foolishness," Bill said in a cold tone that Randy had never heard in his voice before.

"You mean foolishness like saying what we saw was real?"

"That's the kind of foolishness I'm talking about," Bill said. He wouldn't meet Randy's eyes.

"But what if I can prove it to you?" Randy said. He reached into his satchel and pulled out his library book. "I found this book all about real-life monsters and unexplained—" He stumbled over the word *phenomenas*.

"There's all kinds of foolishness that gets wrote down in books," Bill said. "The Russians got books saying that communism is A-OK. There's plenty of communists in America saying the same thing."

Randy wasn't sure how Bill managed to twist every conversation to be about communism. "Wait, I'm confused. Are you saying I'm a communist?"

"I've said you're yellow, but I ain't said you're red," Bill said. "But you said yourself you're confused. And a confused mind is a weak mind. When your mind is weak, you'll let all kinds of dangerous ideas inside it. Until you come around to seeing things with good sense, I think it's better that we don't talk."

They obeyed Bill's wishes the rest of the way. It felt like the longest walk of Randy's life.

As soon as he got home, Randy changed into his work clothes. He gathered eggs and fed the chickens. He fed and watered Maybelle the cow and the pig he called Elvis, even though Momma had said not to name it or get attached to it. He did every chore completely and correctly, but his mind was elsewhere, thinking about Bill's strange behavior but also about the library book that was waiting for him in his room and what kind of answers it might give him.

Once he finished his chores, he hurried back to the house, excited to finally settle down with the book. As soon as he walked in, though, Momma said, "Time to wash up for supper."

"Yes, ma'am," he said, trying not to let his frustration show. He washed his hands in the bathroom sink and splashed some water on his face. He sat down at the table to a meal of pinto beans, corn bread, and fried taters. Now that they had less money, Momma cooked a big pot of beans every Monday and they ate off it all week.

"You feeling better today, Randy?" Momma asked.

Randy was confused. "I ain't been sick."

"I know," Momma said, crumbling corn bread over her beans. "But you was saying some peculiar things yesterday . . . about what you thought you saw. I just wanted to make sure you ain't . . . confused anymore."

"I'm not confused," Randy said. And he wasn't. He knew what he saw.

"That's good," Momma said, smiling over at Daddy. "Ain't it, Charles?"

"It is," Daddy said. He always ate a peeled onion with his soup beans. He didn't slice it, either. He just picked it up and bit into it like an apple. "We can't have the boy going around talking about seeing monsters in the woods. People will think he's crazy as a bess-bug."

"Crazy as a bess-bug," Cindy said, giggling. "That's funny, Daddy."

After supper, Randy excused himself to do homework, though, what he really wanted to do was finally pore over the *Meeting Monsters* book. In his room, he took the book out of his satchel and hid it behind his open history textbook so that anybody who saw him would think he was studying.

He lay propped up on the pillows on his bed and flipped through the book so he could see all the illustrations. There were all kinds of weird critters—one that looked like a cross between a man and a monkey, another that looked like a dinosaur. But he didn't see one single illustration that even vaguely resembled what he was coming to think of as his monster.

The author of the book was a man named

Professor J. Alfred Northrup. He listed a bunch of letters behind his name, too, but Randy didn't know what they meant. In the introduction to the book, Mr. Northrup wrote,

"The mysterious creatures you will meet in these pages are ones I either met myself or heard about on good authority. I do not pretend that this is an exhaustive list of the previously unknown beings in the world or even in the United States. Even as you read, there may be a new mysterious creature that was just discovered, so it cannot grace the pages of this book."

Randy felt a little leap of excitement. What if he and Bill were the only people who had ever seen the monster? What if they were the ones who had *discovered* it?

Cindy came into the room and disappeared behind her curtain for a minute. When she popped over to Randy's side of the room, she was wearing her nightgown. Her eyes looked sleepy. "Whatcha reading?" she asked.

Randy looked down at the book he was hiding with his history textbook. There was no need to lie to Cindy. "A book about monsters."

Now Cindy's eyes were open wide. "What kind of monsters?"

He did need to be careful, though, not to scare her right before her bedtime. "Well, not all of them are monsters. Some of them are just animals nobody knew about before."

"Can I see?" Cindy asked, nodding toward the book.

He handed it to her, and she sat on the edge of his bed and flipped through the pictures. "Are you reading this on account of what you saw out in the woods?" she asked.

Randy, not for the first time, thought about what a smart kid Cindy was. "Yeah. I mean, I guess I'm looking for answers. And it kind of helps me to know that there are other people who've seen things they can't explain. Because nobody I've told about it thinks it's real. Even Bill don't think it's real, and he was right there with me."

Cindy looked up from the book and fixed her gaze on Randy. "Well, I believe you."

It was a huge relief to hear those words. "You do?"

"Sure I do." She closed the book and handed it back to Randy. "Bill got so scared he don't want to believe in it. And grown-ups always say monsters ain't nothing but make-believe, but us kids know better."

Randy smiled. "Is that why you always ask me to check under your bed every night before you go to sleep?"

Cindy nodded. "Uh-huh. Because I know. I know monsters are real."

CHAPTER 5

It had been a week since Randy had talked to anybody about the monster. He and Bill still hadn't made up, although somebody had left a pamphlet titled *How to Spot a Communist* in Randy's locker at school. Did Bill honestly think Randy was a communist just because he didn't believe that the monster they saw was part of some Russian plot?

Right now Randy's only comfort came from two people, Cindy and Professor J. Alfred Northrup, the author of *Meeting Monsters*, which Randy kept close at hand whenever possible.

Tonight he had fallen asleep reading the book. He was overtired. Ever since the incident in the woods, he was plagued by nightmares, sometimes dreams in which the monster appeared, other times ones in which he tried to warn people about the monster, but no one would listen to him or believe him. He always woke up not knowing which was more frightening, the monster itself or the feeling of not being heard.

But right now his sleep was deep and dreamless, a blessing after so many fitful nights.

A green glow poured through the bedroom window. Randy's eyes snapped open.

He didn't know if he had ever gone from asleep to fully awake so quickly. He got out of bed and peeked around the privacy curtain to make sure Cindy was still sleeping. She was. It would take much more than a strange light to wake her when she was good and out. He pushed open the window and climbed through it. He knew he might be in danger, but he was willing to take the risk. He wanted to see the monster again so there would be no doubt it was real.

He stepped outside, his bare feet chilled in the damp grass. He could see the figure at the end of the pasture, floating a few feet above the ground. He looked over at Bill's house and wondered if the green light had also spilled into Bill's window. If so, he saw no signs of Bill coming out to investigate.

Maybelle had, though. She had gotten out of the barn again—how could a stupid cow be such an escape artist?—and was standing in the pasture looking in the monster's, seemingly hypnotized by the green glow.

Making sure to avoid Maybelle's cow pies, Randy trudged across the pasture toward the monster. It looked just as it had before. The green cloak. The obscured face. The huge, red, glowing eyes. There was something ghostly in the way its robe and cape flowed with the wind currents. Randy's heart pounded, and a cold sweat prickled his forehead.

Somehow the monster was scarier here than it was in the woods. Maybe it was because he was facing it alone, or maybe it was because it was encroaching on Randy's territory. This time, Randy didn't find the monster. The monster had found him.

It knew where he lived.

"Hello," Randy said. He tried to speak loudly enough to be heard, but his voice was shaking. "Can you talk?"

The creature said nothing, just floated above him.

"Because I figure you want something, or why else would you be here?"

It floated wordlessly. Randy looked below its robe. He saw no legs, just green-tinted air.

"Wh-what are you?" Randy stammered. "What do you want?"

The creature started to vibrate. Its cloak and robe rippled, and it emitted a low hum that reminded Randy a little of the cicadas that showed up sometimes in the summer. But then the humming felt like it was in

Randy's body, in his blood, and there were no thoughts in his head, no speech on his tongue.

He woke up in his bed, with the usual morning light streaming through the window.

Okay, so it was a dream, Randy told himself. *A real strange dream.*

But when he threw off the covers, he saw the grass and the dirt on his bare feet.

When Randy went into the kitchen, his mother was sitting at the table. At night, Momma always sat in her rocker and sewed while listening to the radio, but Randy could hardly remember ever seeing her sit down during the day. She was always on her feet, busy doing something.

"Momma, are you all right?" Randy said.

Momma looked up at him with tears in her eyes. "Randy, the cow's gone dry. There's no milk. None to drink and none to sell."

Randy's legs felt too weak and shaky to hold him up. He sank into the kitchen chair across from Momma. He thought of the strange vibrations that had come from the monster, that had made him feel like his blood was humming in his veins. Did the monster have this effect on Maybelle, too? Did it cause her to stop making milk? "Maybe she's sick," Randy said weakly.

"Could be," Momma said. "She had that calf we sold after it was weaned. That was just a couple of months ago. She still should have plenty of milk."

"Maybe we ought to call Doc Jenkins." Doc Jenkins was whom you called when an animal was having a hard time giving birth or had some other problem you couldn't figure out how to fix on your own.

"And what would we pay him with?" Momma asked. "You know how I paid Doc Jenkins when we had him out here last time?"

"No, ma'am," Randy said.

"I paid him in milk. Two gallons." Momma laughed, but somehow it wasn't a happy laugh.

Randy joined her. At least laughing helped break some of the tension.

"Your daddy went over to cut some feller's grass early this morning," Momma said, "so I ain't even told him about the cow yet. I don't know if he can stand one more piece of bad luck."

Everything inside Randy wanted to say, *I saw the monster again last night, right in our pasture, and Maybelle was there, too. Maybe it's the monster that's bringing us bad luck.* But he stopped himself. He knew Momma wouldn't believe him, and having a cow that had dried up and a son that imagined things would be more than she could handle. So instead he asked, "Is there anything we can do to doctor up the cow someway ourselves?"

Momma was quiet for a few seconds, then said, "Well, I know what my granny did when a cow dried up. She always said it was because some witch had put a hex on it. She said if you cut off some hairs from the end of the cow's tail, then built a fire and threw the hairs into the flames, it would burn away the hex."

Randy wondered if what the monster did was the same thing as a hex. "You think we should try it?"

Momma smiled sadly and shook her head. "That's just an old wives' tale. Granny was full of them. And besides, you think there's really witches around here?"

No, Randy thought. *But there's a monster.* "I know it seems silly," he said. "But what have we got to lose?"

"Well, nothing, I reckon." Momma got up from the table. "Let me get my scissors and a book of matches."

Randy distracted Maybelle by petting her velvety nose while Momma crept around behind her and cut some hairs from her tail.

"I can't believe you talked me into this," Momma said, holding up a handful of bristly hairs. "We'd better finish this foolishness before your daddy comes home. He's already worried on account of you saying you saw a monster. We don't want him thinking I've started making up stuff, too."

Randy kept silent on the subject of the monster. "You want me to build a fire?" he asked.

Momma nodded.

Randy grabbed a few small pieces of kindling from the woodpile. He made a little nest of firewood, then struck a match and dropped it in the center.

Soon, they were standing over a fire.

"I don't remember if there's some words you're supposed to say when you throw the hairs into the fire," Momma said. "Like if there's a Bible verse or some kind of rhyme. I reckon I'll just throw them in and hope for the best."

The hairs from Maybelle's tail made a sizzling sound when they hit the flames. Randy's nose filled with the unpleasant smell of burned hair.

He and his mother looked at each other like they weren't quite sure why they'd done what they'd just done.

Cindy came running from the house, still in her nightgown. "What in the world are y'all doing?" she asked.

Momma looked at Randy, then said, "Just burning some trash."

"You know what we ought to do?" Cindy said. "We ought to have us a weenie roast."

Momma laughed. "For breakfast?"

"Why can't you have hot dogs for breakfast?" Cindy said.

"Well, I don't reckon there's a law against it," Momma said. "There's a package of weenies in the ice-box. Run and fetch them."

Cindy ran back to the house.

"You want me to find some green sticks?" Randy asked.

Momma nodded.

Randy walked over to the edge of the woods, looking for new branches poking out from the trees. New wood that was still green in the middle wouldn't burn when you held it in the fire. He cut down a couple small branches with his pocketknife, then sharpened their ends into points. He thought over the events of the past hour. The cow had gone dry, he and his mom had done some kind of spell to try to fix it, and now they were going to have hot dogs for breakfast. It had been a strange morning.

Momma, Cindy, and Randy stood around the fire, impaling weenies on their sharp sticks and laughing at the silliness of what they were doing. Randy heard the rumble of Daddy's old truck coming up their long gravel driveway. The truck pulled up right where they were standing, and Daddy rolled down the window. "Now, what in the Sam Hill is going on here?" he asked, but he didn't sound angry, just curious.

"We're roasting weenies for breakfast! You want one?" Cindy said with a giggle in her voice.

Daddy laughed and shook his head. "Sure. Why the heck not?"

CHAPTER 6

The next morning, Randy woke up to find Momma busying around the kitchen as usual. The whole house smelled of coffee and bacon. "You want one egg or two?" Momma asked. Yesterday's heaviness was gone from her voice and body.

"Two, please," Randy said, sitting down at the table.

Cindy was already at the table, mopping up egg yolk with a biscuit. "I had three!" she said.

"Your sister's getting to be as hard to fill up as you are," Momma said. She set down a glass of milk on the table in front of Randy. "There's plenty of milk this morning, by the way."

Randy couldn't hide his surprise. "Really? You reckon what we did worked?"

"Could be," Momma said. "All I know is that Maybelle's udders is back in business."

"What did you do?" Cindy said.

Momma gave Randy a *Don't say anything* look. "We just said some prayers for Maybelle. She wasn't feeling good yesterday, so she wasn't giving no milk."

"I want to say a prayer for Maybelle, too," Cindy said.

"You can any time you want to," Momma said. "I'm sure she'd appreciate it."

Randy's brain was going too fast to follow the conversation around him. Did the monster cause Maybelle to stop giving milk? Had the weird charm he and Momma had done yesterday caused Maybelle's milk to come back? Or was everything just a coincidence? Not long ago, Randy had thought that life followed a logical order. He thought that you could always figure out causes and effects so everything came out nice and neat like an arithmetic problem. Now he knew he'd been wrong. Why his dad had lost his job, why the monster had appeared to him, why Bill had decided he didn't want to be friends anymore . . . none of these were questions he could answer.

Even though Bill didn't come over anymore to walk with him to the bus, there was no way to avoid him on the walk out of the holler. Bill was walking silently, staring straight ahead, like a horse with blinders on.

Randy decided to take his chances and greet him like everything was normal. "Hey, Bill."

Bill didn't say anything, didn't even turn his head.

"So we still ain't talking? Is that it?" Randy said.

"You're talking," Bill said, still not looking at him. "I don't reckon I can stop you from talking."

You're talking now, too, Randy thought, but he knew better than to say it. Instead he said, "I don't understand why you're sore at me."

"I ain't sore at you," Bill said. "You just ain't the person I thought you was, is all."

"And what person did you think I was?"

"Somebody with good sense!" Bill said. He was looking at Randy now, and his expression was angry. "Somebody who wouldn't be out doing witchcraft with his momma in broad daylight. Someone who wouldn't fall hook, line, and sinker for a piece of communist propaganda!"

Randy sighed. Bill must have seen him and Momma from his window. "Me and Momma wasn't doing witchcraft. It was some superstition she learned from her momma about what to do when a cow dries up."

"Well, women pass down witchcraft through the generations," Bill said as though he was being completely logical.

"Let me get this straight. You're saying my momma is a witch, and you're saying the monster was a piece of communist propaganda?" Randy asked. He wasn't even sure what propaganda was, but he was pretty sure the monster wasn't an example of it.

"That's right, and you believe all that stuff is real," Bill said. "You're playing right into their hands. You're probably already a member of the party for all I know."

Randy threw up his hands in exasperation. "Bill, that's the most harebrained thing I've ever heard. I am not a communist!"

Bill looked at him with narrowed eyes. "That's exactly what a communist would say."

Randy sighed as they approached the school bus. "Well, there's no sense arguing with you." He stepped up onto the bus.

"That's just what I was about to say," Bill said, getting on right behind him. He leaned over and hissed so only Randy could hear him, "From now on, just stay away from me. I ain't got time for no communist sons of witches."

Randy sat on the school bus alone, with only the words of Professor J. Alfred Northrup for companionship.

School was a misery. In study hall, Randy hunched over his notebook and tried to draw the most accurate picture he could of the monster. He wasn't a great artist, but the monster wasn't hard to draw—a head peaked from its hood, the floating robe and cloak, the enormous eyes. He drew squiggles around it to represent the glow radiating from its body.

"Hey, that's pretty good," a voice from over his shoulder said. "An alien, right?"

Randy looked up to see the source of the voice. It was the new kid, James, the one nobody ever talked to because everybody said he was weird.

"Thanks," Randy said. "Yeah, it could be an alien."

"Oh, it's definitely an alien," James said. He wore thick glasses, and his nose and cheeks were spotted with large freckles. "I've read accounts from people who have spotted aliens that looked just like this." He sat down at the desk next to Randy's and picked up the picture to inspect it more closely.

"You believe in them—aliens, spacemen, that kind of thing?" Randy asked.

"Sure," James said, handing Randy the picture back. "Like what happened in Roswell, New Mexico, back in '47 when they found that crashed flying disk? The government cleaned it up, of course, buried the aliens' bodies, came up with some phony-baloney story about the spaceship being a weather balloon. That's just what the government wants you to think."

James talking about the government reminded Randy of Bill talking about communists; however, he was intrigued that somebody might be willing to listen to his story without judging him. "So have you ever seen an alien?" Randy asked.

James grinned. He had a pronounced overbite. "No, I'd love to, though. I wouldn't be scared. I'd just want to talk to the aliens and find out what they know that we don't."

"I saw one," Randy whispered. "At least I think that's what I saw."

"Did it look like that?" James nodded in the direction of Randy's drawing.

Randy nodded.

"Where was it? Was it around here?" James's eyes were wide behind his glasses. He was quivering with excitement.

"Yeah, in the woods near the bottom of Green Mountain. I saw it when me and a buddy of mine was camping out there one night."

"Did you get any pictures of it?"

"No. I don't have a camera," Randy said. Even if he did, he probably wouldn't have taken it with him on the camping trip. He hadn't been expecting to see anything unusual.

"You've got to go back to the original site!" James said. He was becoming more and more animated. "You need to go around the same time you saw it before and see if it shows up again."

Randy thought of his and Bill's abandoned campsite. He hadn't even gone back there to get his blanket. "That's not a bad idea."

James nodded. "And I've got a good camera. You could take me with you. I could document it for posterity."

Randy looked at the eager expression on the strange kid's face. He seemed harmless enough. And besides, Randy was lonely. "Sure, you can come. If my parents say it's okay for you to sleep over on Saturday night. But we're sleeping in the house. No more camping out on the mountain for me."

"I would be delighted to sleep over at your house! This is the first time anybody's invited me over since I moved here from Cincinnati. I'm James, by the way." He held out his hand for Randy to shake.

Randy already knew the kid's name, of course. He and Bill had talked the night they camped out about how weird he was. But he held his hand out to James as though, before now, he hadn't known him from Adam. "Good to meet you. I'm Randy."

CHAPTER 7

Randy had been waiting most of the evening for a good time to ask his parents if James could spend the night on Saturday. It was an unusual request. Nobody had ever slept over at their house but Bill, and Randy had known Bill his whole life.

He waited until Momma and Daddy seemed relaxed. Cindy had gone to bed, and Momma and Daddy were sitting by the radio. Momma was sewing, and Daddy was whittling on a piece of wood, probably carving it into some little animal for Cindy. Even when they were relaxing, Momma and Daddy kept their hands busy.

He made sure not to bother them until a commercial came on the radio. Sometimes Daddy got irritated if you interrupted a program he liked. When he heard a jingle for headache powders, he finally approached them. "Momma, Daddy, I want to ask you something."

"Well, let's see if we can answer it," Daddy said, carving off a long wood shaving with his pocketknife.

Randy smiled nervously. "So there's this boy at school, James. I've been talking to him, and he's real nice. I was wondering if he could spend the night on Saturday."

"Who's his people?" Momma asked.

"I don't really know," Randy said, mad at himself for not anticipating this question. "He just moved here from Cincinnati."

Momma and Daddy exchanged a glance. To them, big cities were always scary places, full of the violence that comes from people living close together like rats in cages.

"His daddy is the new pharmacist at the drug-store," Randy said quickly, hoping that this respectable job might help his case.

"Huh," Daddy said. "I bet your new friend lives in a fancy house in town. He ain't gonna be used to a poor folks' house like ours."

"He don't care about our house, Daddy," Randy said. *He cares about seeing the monster.* But of course Randy couldn't say this.

"Where would you sleep?" Momma asked. "You'uns can't sleep in there with Cindy."

"I figure if it's a nice night we can sleep on the

porch," Randy said. "If it rains, we'll make pallets on the floor of the living room."

Momma sighed. "Well, give me his mother's phone number. I'll call her tomorrow. If she seems all right and if it's all right with your daddy, he can come stay."

"I'll leave it up to you," Daddy said to Momma. "I trust your judgment."

Randy had known Momma would ask for James's mother's phone number. He had been carrying a slip of paper with the number on it in his pocket all day. He handed it to her.

Things looked hopeful. They hadn't said no, and usually, if they didn't say no right away, it meant they were on their way to a yes.

"It's so pretty out here," James said after his mother had let him out of her shiny, new-looking car. "I bet it's spooky at night, though."

Randy had never thought of where he lived as spooky . . . not until the monster showed up, anyway. "Well, I reckon you'll get to be the judge of that after it gets dark," Randy said.

Momma had confessed to Randy that she was nervous about what kinds of food a boy from Cincinnati might eat, so she had gone to the store in town and splurged on white bread and peanut butter and cheese and potato chips, treats that she usually said were too expensive and too silly to buy.

When they all sat around the table together, Randy's parents looked at James like he was as strange as the monster in the woods. "Is the food all right?" Momma asked.

"Sure," James said, taking a big rabbity bite of his sandwich. "This is the best grape jelly I've ever had."

Momma gave a rare smile. "Oh, I made that myself. I put it up this summer."

"Wow," James said. "I didn't know people could make jelly."

Daddy laughed, but it sounded good-natured. "Well, who did you think made jelly, son? Elves?"

James grinned. "No, I just thought . . . factories made it."

"I think elves should make it," Cindy said, giggling. "Like the elves that work for Santa."

Now everybody was laughing.

Randy had been a little nervous about how James would fit in with his family, but now he felt relieved and happy that everybody was getting along.

After supper, James went with Randy to help gather eggs.

"I've never been around chickens before," James said.

Randy grinned. "Did you think eggs was made in a factory, too?"

"No, I knew chickens laid them. I've just never known any chickens personally."

Randy showed James how to gently reach under the hens and retrieve an egg.

"Do they mind it?" James asked. "I wouldn't want somebody reaching under me like that."

Randy laughed. "They're used to it. Aren't you, Anne Francis?"

"After the actress from *Forbidden Planet*?" James asked

"Yeah," Randy said, surprised and pleased that James had gotten the reference. "And this is Zsa Zsa and Eva, and that mean rooster over there is Godzilla."

James nodded his approval. "I love Godzilla. Anything with a monster in it, I'm in." He looked into the distance. "So, speaking of monsters, the monster you saw showed up in those woods?"

Randy nodded. "I'd say about a quarter mile up the mountain." Randy thought of that night in the woods with Bill. He looked over at Bill's house and wondered if Bill had looked out his window and caught a glimpse of Randy and his new friend. Randy felt a pang. He guessed that Bill wasn't his best friend after all.

"What time do you think he'll show up?"

"I don't know if he will or he won't," Randy said.

Come to think of it, he didn't even know if the monster was a *he* or not. "But if it does show up, I don't think it'll be until after full dark. Oh, and we'll have to be careful about going up there. I haven't exactly told Momma and Daddy that we're going into the woods."

James looked at Randy and nodded. "A secret mission. I gotcha."

The secret mission got underway around 11 p.m. after everybody else was asleep. Because it would make less noise than opening the creaky door, Randy and James tiptoed into Randy's room and climbed out the window. Randy had a flashlight in hand, and James was carrying a knapsack bulging with what he called his monster-hunting supplies.

"I'm afraid it's gonna be too dark to get a good picture, but I'm still gonna try," James said.

"Well, don't get your hopes up too high," Randy said. "We don't even know if the thing is gonna show up."

"I know there are no guarantees," James said. "But I still think it will. I just have a feeling, you know?"

Randy didn't want to admit it, but he had a feeling, too. Maybe he was wrong, but he felt like the monster was drawn to him somehow. Like it wanted to see him, wanted something from him. But what?

Is that why the monster had made Maybelle's milk dry up? To punish Randy for not giving it whatever it was that it wanted? Or was he just trying to make connections where there weren't any?

Either way, he hoped the monster showed up so James could see it. If somebody else saw it and agreed that it was real, he would feel a whole lot better about things.

They had reached the edge of the woods. "You'll want to use your flashlight and watch where you walk," Randy said. "There's lots of roots and rocks to trip over."

From watching James trying to negotiate the mountain, it was obvious he was a flatlander. He stumbled more than he stepped and kept grabbing on to trees for support. "You want to take my arm to steady you?" Randy asked.

"Sure. Thanks. I've never done anything like this before." There was unmistakable excitement in James's voice. "Usually my idea of living dangerously is reading comic books with a flashlight under the covers after bedtime and hoping my mom doesn't catch me."

Randy grinned. He was starting to genuinely like James. Sure, he was different, but different was interesting. "Well, grab hold of my arm, then. It's one thing to live dangerously, but it's another to fall down and break your neck."

Together they made their way up the base of the mountain.

It was spooky when they arrived at Randy and Bill's old campsite. Despite a few signs of rain and wear and tear, everything was just like they had left it. There was the little pile of wood that had been their campfire. The pup tent, which Randy thought Bill might have gone back for in daylight, was still standing.

"This is it," Randy said.

"This is where the monster appeared?" James asked, looking around.

Randy pointed into the air in front of them. "It was right here, floating just above us."

"Wow," James said. "So is there anything we can do to make it show up—any way we can lure it?"

"I don't reckon," Randy said. "Before, it showed up when we was asleep. I guess all we can do is wait."

They sat on the cool ground and waited. James took his camera out of his satchel so he'd be ready in case the monster materialized.

"What do you think it is?" James asked. "An alien?"

"Maybe," Randy said. "I guess it could be a ghost from the way it kinda floats. But I tend to just call it the Monster when I think about it."

"The Green Mountain Monster," James said. "That would be a good name for it. Like if we get credit for discovering it."

"That is a good name," Randy said. "Has a nice ring to it."

"Yeah. But if it looks like the thing you were drawing, it's definitely an alien."

They talked for a while, but it was late and dark, and before long the boys started to doze. An hour passed, and then Randy felt a strange green glow penetrate his eyelids. "Wake up," he whispered. "It's here."

James was awake and on his feet in record time. Randy stood more slowly, then looked up at the floating green figure with red headlight-like eyes.

"Whoa." James breathed.

"Hello again," Randy said, looking up at the figure, his heart pounding. It turned its red gaze on him. "I don't know why you keep showing up where I am, but if there's some way you want me to help you, I'll do it. We're just gonna have to figure out some way to talk to each other. You can't talk like we can, can you?"

The creature hovered silently.

"Dark or not, I've got to try to get a picture of this," James said. He raised up his camera and aimed it at the monster. Before he could push the button, the camera flew out of his hands. For a few seconds, it soared crazily over the boys' heads, just out of their reach. Then it smashed into a tree and fell to the ground in pieces.

Well, Randy thought, *that's one way the monster is getting his ideas across.* When he looked up from the broken camera, the monster was gone.

CHAPTER 8

I can't believe it," James said for the twelfth time since they started their walk back down. "I mean, I believe it, but I can't believe it, you know?"

"I know," Randy said. They were in the pasture now. "Watch out for cow pies."

"What are cow pies?"

Randy shook his head. James was such a city boy. "Cow dung," he said. "Poop."

"Do they just poop out in the fields?" James asked.

"What, you expect them to have their own special cow toilets?" Randy said, laughing.

When they got near the house, Randy was surprised to see a shiny black car in the driveway. It was such a strange sight at this late hour that it took him a couple of seconds to recognize whose car it was. Doc

Carter. And if Doc Carter was here, it was because something had gone wrong—so wrong that it couldn't wait until the morning. Worry prickled Randy's stomach. Had Cindy gotten sick, maybe spiked up a high fever? But she had been fine when they'd left to go to the woods, and they hadn't been gone that long.

Momma met them at the door. "Where in the Sam Hill have you been?" Her face was a mask of worry.

"We just went to the woods," Randy said. He hoped Momma didn't fuss at him too much, not in front of his new friend. It was embarrassing.

"You know you ain't supposed to go to the woods and not tell your daddy and me where you're going," Momma said.

"I know," Randy said. Momma was right. He should have told her. He had just gotten all caught up in the idea of having a secret adventure. "I'm sorry."

"I needed help with your daddy," Momma said, her voice threatening to break into a sob. "And I couldn't find you."

A wave of fear washed over Randy. He hadn't even considered that the doctor could be there because of Daddy. "What's the matter with Daddy?"

Momma cast a worried glance back inside the house. "He couldn't sleep and decided to go outside for some air like he does sometimes. He went out on the back steps, and the top step just broke under his weight. It was the strangest thing. The wood wasn't rotted or nothing. He landed wrong when he fell, and when he tried to get up, he couldn't stand on his right leg. Doc Carter says it's broke."

A shiver passed over Randy. The last time he had seen the monster, Maybelle had stopped giving milk. This time Daddy had broken his leg. *Coincidences*, Randy tried to tell himself. *But are they?* "I'm sorry," Randy said again. "I'm sorry I wasn't there to help when it happened."

"Probably not much you could've done anyway," Momma said. "Come on in the house. Your daddy and me are gonna follow Doc into town to the infirmary. He's got the stuff he needs to make a cast for your daddy's leg there. It's gonna be a long night. You boys stay here with Cindy, all right?"

"Yes, ma'am," Randy said.

Daddy was lying on the couch with his hurt leg propped up. "Hidy, boys," he said. He was trying to sound friendly and cheerful, but Randy could hear the pain in his voice. "Never managed to get myself hurt in ten years of working in the mines, then I break my leg on my own back steps."

"That's how it goes," Doc Carter said. He was the only doctor in Green Mountain and had delivered Randy and his sister. With a full head of gray hair, he looked old, but at the same time he never seemed to age.

"People get hurt when they least expect it. Boys, could you help me get our patient out to the truck?"

"Yes, sir," Randy said. He and James stood on either side of Daddy and steadied him as he awkwardly hopped on one foot toward the front door. They helped him into the truck's passenger seat, and Momma slid in on the driver's side.

It was only after they'd gotten Daddy safely into the truck that the consequences of Daddy's accident started to dawn on Randy. With his right leg in a cast, Daddy wouldn't be able to drive. With a broken leg, he wouldn't be able to do the odd jobs he had cobbled together since losing his job in the mines. No odd jobs meant no money, except for the little bit Momma brought in selling milk and eggs. Randy was going to have to find a way to earn some money, too, or they weren't going to make enough to put food on the table.

"Randy?" James's voice penetrated Randy's thoughts.

"Yeah?"

"That was the third time I said your name," James said, but he didn't sound mad, just matter of fact.

"I'm sorry," Randy said. "What happened just now . . . it was all kind of a lot to take in."

"I know," James said, following Randy back into the house. "I'm sorry your dad got hurt."

"Me too," Randy said. Feeling overcome by

exhaustion suddenly, he sat down on the couch. James sat down beside him.

"If you think your parents would rather I not be here, I can call my mom to pick me up," James said.

"No." The word came out almost too forcefully. "Stay. I'd feel weird sitting here by myself." Randy paused. "James?"

"Yeah?"

"What if the monster—or the alien or whatever it is—wants to hurt me and my family?" He knew there was nobody else in the world he could say this to but James, the only other person he knew who had seen the monster and believed in it.

"What do you mean?" James asked, looking at him intently through his thick glasses.

"Well, every time I've seen the monster, something bad's happened right after. After the first time I saw it, Bill stopped being my friend. After the next time, our cow stopped giving milk. And this time, Daddy broke his leg. I mean, there's only so many times you can call something a coincidence."

"But why would the monster choose you to pick on?" James asked. "I mean, of all the people in the world it could cause bad luck, why would it choose some kid in the middle of nowhere in West Virginia?"

"I don't know," Randy said. "It doesn't make sense. But some things don't, you know? Maybe we shouldn't even be asking why. Maybe some things are just supposed to stay—" He lost his words. He really was very tired.

"Mysterious? Unexplained?" James finished for him. Randy nodded. "Yeah, like that."

"I hope you're wrong about it," James said. "I want it to be a friendly visitor from another planet, not a monster who hurts people. But whatever it is, it's the most amazing thing I've ever seen. It was worth losing my camera just to get to lay eyes on it. Thanks for taking me up there."

"I'm glad you went," Randy said. "I needed for somebody else to see it with me. Somebody who wouldn't talk themselves out of believing what they'd seen. I'll tell you what, though. I ain't gonna go looking for that thing anymore. If it wants me, it has to come find me its own self."

CHAPTER 9

"Here's today's earnings," Randy said, setting five one-dollar bills down on the kitchen table.

"Thank you, honey. That helps a lot," Momma said, stirring up the batter for corn bread.

"You're a good boy," Daddy said from his spot lying on the couch. "I just hate being laid up like this. And I hate sending a boy to do a man's job."

"I wish I could do more," Randy said. "It's just hard with school." Since Daddy broke his leg a couple of weeks ago, Randy had taken up all the odd jobs he could find in walking distance. He cleaned out one neighbor's barn and cut another neighbor's grass. An old lady who lived right outside the holler was going to pay him to paint her porch on Saturday.

"Well, school's the most important thing," Momma

said. "You've got to work hard and stay in school so you'll have opportunities your daddy and me never had. Who knows? You might be the first in our family to go to college."

"That's right," Daddy said. "Then you can make the big bucks and take care of me in my old age."

Cindy rushed into the room, her eyes big and shiny like they got when she was excited. "I'm gonna help make money, too, Daddy! I'm gonna open up a lemonade stand."

"I think that's a real nice idea, honey," Momma said. She bent over to slide the cast-iron skillet of sizzling corn-bread batter into the oven.

"Where are you gonna have this lemonade stand, Cindy?" Randy asked.

"Out in the front yard," Cindy said.

Randy felt the need to reason with her, though, he wasn't sure that reasoning would work. "But we live so far away from a main road that nobody's gonna see your lemonade stand. Who's gonna buy the lemonade?"

Cindy looked at him like he was making no sense. "Well, you and Momma and Daddy."

"But that's not really making money for the family, is it?" Randy said. "That's just handing you some money you'll hand right back to us."

Cindy narrowed her eyes. "Are you saying I can't have me a lemonade stand?"

"No," Randy said. "I'm just saying—"

"Of course you can have you a lemonade stand, Cindy Bug," Daddy said, cutting Randy off. "I'd love to try a glass of your lemonade. And it's real sweet that you want to help out."

Randy could hear the sadness in Daddy's voice. Even though it couldn't be helped, Randy knew it was hard for Daddy to lie around every day unable to work to feed his family. Randy knew that Daddy's leg hurt, but he suspected that Daddy's pride hurt even more.

The next day at school, Randy sat with James in the lunchroom. Bill, he noticed, was sitting with the same table full of boys he had been sitting with since their falling-out.

"Who are you looking at?" James said.

"Oh, nobody. I was just thinking," Randy said. But not only had he seen Bill, he had seen Bill looking back at him with a searching expression on his face, like he had lost something and was hoping to find it.

"Were you thinking about the Green Mountain Monster?" James asked, unwrapping his sandwich. Peanut butter and jelly, from the looks of it.

"Yeah, kind of."

"I think when we talk about it, we should always

call it the Green Mountain Monster. That way, we'll get credit for discovering it and naming it." He bit into his sandwich and chewed thoughtfully. "Though, really, you should probably get credit for discovering it, and I should get credit for naming it. That's probably fairer since you saw it first."

"What do you mean by 'credit'?" Randy asked. James had been talking very fast, and he was pretty sure he had missed something important.

"I mean when we go to the press and tell our story," James said. "It'll put Green Mountain on the map, that's for sure."

Suddenly, James felt too nervous to eat his cold bacon biscuit. "I don't know that I want to tell anybody. Momma and Daddy didn't believe me when I told them about the monster. Why should I think a newspaper reporter would believe me?"

"Simple," James said, opening his carton of milk. "Because they want to sell newspapers."

"Yeah, I guess," Randy said. "But I feel like if I was in the newspaper as the kid who saw a monster, it would embarrass my family."

"They'd get over it," James said. He stuffed the uneaten crusts from his sandwich into his lunch sack. "They have to. They're your family."

"Maybe," Randy said. "I don't know. I need to think about it more."

"Fair enough," James said. "But you know how you were saying you didn't know what the monster wanted from you?"

"Uh-huh."

"Maybe it wants you to tell its story."

When Randy got off the school bus, Bill surprised him by walking up beside him.

"Hey," Bill said.

"Hey," Randy answered cautiously.

"I've seen you with that James kid a lot," Bill said, almost like he was accusing Randy of doing something wrong.

"Yeah? So?" They had fallen into walking together, but it didn't feel comfortable like the old days.

Bill shrugged. "Nothing."

"So I'm not supposed to have other friends now that you don't want to have anything to do with me?"

Bill shoved his hands into his pockets. "Well, it's none of my business, I guess. He's just kind of a weird kid is all."

"You're right. It is none of your business."

They walked for a few minutes in uncomfortable silence.

"He's from a big city, you know. Lots of communists

in big cities. Plus, he believes in all that monster stuff," Bill said finally. "He's always talking about it."

"Yeah, and you should believe it, too. You saw the same thing I saw."

"I told you what it was we saw," Bill said. He kept his voice low, but Randy could still hear a sharp edge of anger in it.

"Bill, I'm not gonna have this argument with you again," Randy said. "You're as stubborn as a mule, and nothing I say is gonna change your mind. But I will say that I don't think James talking about monsters all the time is any weirder than the way you're always talking about communists."

Bill laughed, but somehow it didn't seem like a good-natured laugh. "Monsters is make-believe, and communists is real. They don't show us safety films in school about what to do if the monsters attack. It's not weird to worry about real-life things. You and your new best buddy James just wait and see who gets us first, the monsters or the communists."

CHAPTER 10

"Excuse me, you're Randy Siler, right?"

It took Randy a second to place the mustached, middle-aged man who approached him as he walked out the school building toward the bus. "You work for the newspaper, don't you?" Randy finally asked.

The man grinned. The pocket of his rumpled button-down shirt was stuffed full of ink pens, one of which seemed to have sprung a leak. "Work for the newspaper? Heck, I *am* the newspaper." He held out his hand. "Eddie Mathis. Call me Eddie. I went to school with your momma. I was three years ahead of her."

When Momma and Daddy read *The Green Mountain Ledger*, Momma would sometimes mention going to school with the editor. She always said he was the smartest kid in school, but very nice, too, and that he had gotten a full scholarship to West Virginia University. After he graduated, to everybody's surprise, he came back to Green Mountain to take over the local newspaper, which had been in danger of going out of business.

"I've heard her mention you," Randy said.

"Nothing too embarrassing, I hope." His grin showed no sign of fading.

"No, sir."

"Listen," Eddie said in a getting-down-to-business tone. "Your friend James Evans came into my office to talk to me about something y'all saw in the woods the other night. He said it was something you'd seen before, that you had wanted to show it to him."

Randy felt a sudden urge to flee. "I'm going to miss the bus, sir."

"I tell you what," Eddie said. "How about I take you down to the drugstore for a milkshake, and you and I can talk for thirty minutes about what you saw. After that, I can drive you home. Or if you decide you're not comfortable riding with me, I can call your momma to come and get you."

"I don't know, sir," Randy said. He felt shaky all over. "I don't know if I want to say anything that'll get in the newspaper. Except for James, who saw it with his own eyes, and my little sister, nobody I've told about it believes me."

Eddie put his hand on Randy's shoulder. "I believe you, Randy. I can tell you're a truthful boy—not just one who's out to get attention. I wasn't sure about your friend James, but I am sure about you. I believe you're telling the truth, and if you let me write this story, I promise I'm not going to paint you like some kind of crackpot. People need to know the truth, Randy."

It was a relief to be believed by an adult. The only words Randy could find were *thank you*.

"You're welcome, son," Eddie said, clapping him on the back. "Now, are you gonna let me buy you that milkshake or not?"

"Yes, sir," Randy said, smiling. "Thank you." It had been a long time since he'd had a milkshake.

They settled into a booth in the back corner of the Soda Fountain. The place was full of high school kids. Girls with ponytails and scarves and boys with buzz cuts and letter sweaters fed nickels into the jukebox, drank Cokes, and flirted with one another. Randy noted the shiny newness of their saddle oxfords and penny loafers and felt self-conscious about his own beat-up work boots. These weren't the sons and daughters of laid-off coal miners. These were town kids with some spend-ing money.

Eddie took out a notebook and grabbed one of the pens from his pocket. "Don't worry about these older kids being around," he said. "They're paying attention to one another, not to us."

The waitress, the cute older sister of a boy in Randy's class, set down two milkshakes, chocolate for Randy and vanilla for Eddie, in pretty, fluted glasses, each topped with whipped cream and a maraschino cherry.

"Look at that!" Eddie said. "It's a work of art."

The waitress gave a shy smile before leaving them. For a minute, they silently sucked on their straws. When a milkshake was good and thick, it always took a while for it to start flowing upward into your mouth. Once Randy finally got a cold, creamy mouthful, he smiled. "That's real good."

"Mine is, too," Eddie said. "So are you ready to tell me about this monster?"

Randy nodded. "I'll try. I just . . . I don't know where to start."

Eddie's pen was poised above his notepad. "Start at the beginning."

Randy took a deep breath and started.

Friday afternoon, when Randy got home from school, Daddy, from his station on the couch, held up the new issue of *The Green Mountain Ledger*. "I'd like you to explain this to me," Daddy said.

Momma busied herself with sweeping the floor and wouldn't meet Randy's eyes.

With a trembling hand, Randy took the newspaper from Daddy and sank into a chair to read.

UNEXPLAINED PRESENCE LURKS ON GREEN MOUNTAIN, LOCAL BOYS SAY

According to thirteen-year-old Randy Siler and his classmate James Evans, a strange presence haunts the woods of Green Mountain. "I saw it for the first time when I was camping out with a friend," Siler reports. "First there was a strange green glow that woke us up. When we got out of the tent, we saw it. It was bigger than a full-grown man, and it was floating above us. It seemed like it was wearing a green hooded cloak, and you couldn't make out much about its face except that it had these big red glowing eyes . . ."

Randy looked up to see that Momma and Daddy were watching him read. Okay, the truth was out. Now it was time to deal with the consequences.

"Well, you've just about embarrassed your poor mother to death," Daddy said.

It was a strange idea—to be so embarrassed that you actually died.

"It's true," Momma said. "I don't know how I'm gonna show my face in town. I know Eddie Mathis. I can't believe that he'd encourage a child's fairy tales and print trash like this!"

"It's not a fairy tale, Momma. It's the truth. You two always told me the truth would set me free."

Daddy and Momma cast a glance at each other that looked nervous.

"Son, I don't believe you're lying," Daddy said. "I believe you *think* you're telling the truth. But I do believe you're confused in your thoughts, and I think that newspaper man took advantage of you to sell papers. If my leg wasn't broke, I'd march downtown and give him a piece of my mind."

"What do you mean I'm confused in my thoughts?" Randy said, though he was afraid he knew the answer.

"All I mean," Daddy said, "is a person's mind plays tricks on them sometimes. I saw it when I was down in the mines. Being in the dark like that all day does strange things to you. Sometimes fellers would think they saw or heard things that just wasn't there."

Momma shook her head. "This is all people are gonna be talking about till kingdom come. This family's never gonna live it down."

Cindy came in from playing outside. She looked around. "Never gonna live what down?"

Randy was always impressed by how fast Cindy could take the temperature of a room. "You might as well know this, too, Cindy," Randy said. "I told the editor of *The Green Mountain Ledger* about the monster, and the story's in the paper today."

Cindy's eyes widened. "Can I see?"

"Sure. Why not?" Randy handed her the paper.

Cindy couldn't read most words yet, but she put her finger on a spot in the first paragraph and sounded out, "*Rand-ee Sigh-ler.* Wow, Randy, you're famous!"

CHAPTER 11

"Look out, Siler! It's the Green Mountain Monster!" one of the rich boys from town yelled as Randy walked down the hall at school. He had only been at school for an hour, and this was already the twelfth time somebody had yelled something along those lines.

Randy kept his head down and didn't give the kid the satisfaction of a response. He just trudged on toward his locker to get his book for English class. But when he pulled open the door, the locker was empty. Taped to the door was a note on lined paper reading, *The contents of this locker are now the property of the Green Mountain Monster.*

Randy swallowed hard. He had had homework and notes he needed to study in there. Plus, if you lost a textbook, you had to pay the school back for it, and those books didn't come cheap. Part of him wished he could just go home, but things at home weren't easy now, either. He had no choice but to go on to English with no book.

He sat down next to James in class and noticed there was no book on James's desk. "Did somebody swipe your book, too?" Randy asked.

James rolled his eyes. "Yeah," he said. "The Green Mountain Monster, apparently."

Miss Honeycutt took attendance, making eye contact with each student. She was an almost painfully thin middle-aged woman who wore her graying hair in braids pinned to the top of her head. She had moved to Green Mountain from Ohio, and a lot of the kids thought she was stuck up.

After she finished with attendance, Miss Honeycutt looked around the room and said, "Well, it seems we have some celebrities in our midst." She held up a copy of *The Green Mountain Ledger*. "Randy Siler and James Evans, your illustrious classmates, have apparently spotted a monster." She looked at Randy, then at James. "Would either of you gentlemen like to comment on the story?"

Randy looked down at his desk and mumbled, "No, ma'am."

James said, "There's no need for further comment, ma'am. The story's all there in black and white."

James's tone was confident, almost proud. It

occurred to Randy that James was enjoying the attention, even the negative attention.

"I see," Miss Honeycutt said, setting the newspaper down on her desk. "Reading the story, I was reminded of another story, one some of you perhaps read back in elementary school. Does anyone remember the story of 'The Boy Who Cried Wolf'?"

Gladys Newman's hand shot into the air. She was always the first student in class with an answer.

"You remember the story, Gladys?" Miss Honeycutt asked. "Why don't you summarize it for us, please?"

"Yes, ma'am," Gladys said, smiling with the pleasure of a show-off. "In the fable 'The Boy Who Cried Wolf,' a shepherd boy keeps saying a wolf is attacking the flock of sheep he's watching. Each time, somebody comes to check on the sheep, and there is no wolf. But at the end of the story, a wolf really does come, and when the boy tries to tell the people in the village, they don't believe him, and all the sheep get eaten."

"Very good, Gladys," Miss Honeycutt said. Randy could tell that Miss Honeycutt liked Gladys. Probably she had been a lot like Gladys when she was in school. "Now," Miss Honeycutt said, "you said that 'The Boy Who Cried Wolf' is a fable. A fable is a story with a moral lesson. What is the moral lesson of 'The Boy Who Cried Wolf,' Gladys?"

"The moral of the story," Gladys said, "is that if

you keep telling lies, nobody will believe you, even when you're telling the truth."

Miss Honeycutt nodded. "Exactly right, Gladys. What an excellent moral for everyone in this class to keep in mind, whether they're crying *wolf* or *monster.*"

Even though Randy wasn't looking at Miss Honeycutt, he could still feel her gaze. He glanced across the room to where Bill was sitting. Bill should have defended him. He might disagree with Randy about what they saw, but he knew they saw *something.*

But Bill wouldn't meet his eyes. He just stared down at his desk as if it were the most interesting thing in the world.

"Now," Miss Honeycutt said, "if you will get out your pencils and papers, we will begin diagramming sentences."

As Randy and James filed out of the classroom, Randy said, "Boy, I'm gonna be glad when this day is over."

"Why's that?" James said. He sounded genuinely puzzled.

"Well, I mean, you've been having the same day I've been having," Randy said. "People yelling at you and picking on you. Getting your stuff stolen. Being made into some kind of bad example by Miss Honeycutt."

The Chatelaine

"Oh, it's not that bad," James said. "Since when have you cared what Honeycutt thinks?"

"I don't care what she thinks, but it's still embarrassing being singled out in front of the whole class."

James was wearing a strange smile. "See, I feel kind of the opposite. Before we got the story in the paper, nobody talked about me, let alone talked to me. I felt like people here didn't even *see* me. But they see me now, and they can't stop talking about me!"

"Yeah, because they think you're a crackpot or a liar!"

"But at least they have an opinion of me. At least I count. Say, did you ever read *The Picture of Dorian Gray*? It's a really good spooky story."

"No, why?" Randy asked, not sure why James was changing the subject.

"There's a line in that story: *'There is only one thing in the world worse than being talked about, and that is not being talked about.'* The way I figure it, at least I'm being talked about. That's an improvement, right?"

Randy wasn't so sure.

When Randy came out of the school building, the first person he saw was Eddie Mathis, leaning against his car. He smiled and gave Randy a friendly wave.

Randy nodded at him but continued walking toward the bus.

"Randy, could I have a moment of your time, please?" Eddie asked. "How about you skip the bus today and let me give you a ride home?"

Randy couldn't turn down the opportunity of missing the torment he was sure to experience on the bus. "Okay."

Once he was in the car, Eddie said, "*Huge*, Randy. This story is getting to be *huge*. *The Herald-Dispatch* in Huntington and *The Cincinnati Enquirer* have picked it up for their Sunday editions. I figure *The Washington Post* will be next. I'm not sure Green Mountain can handle the fame!" He sounded happy and excited, almost childlike.

"I'm not sure I can handle the fame," Randy said.

"Yeah," Eddie said as they drove away from the school. "I figured today might have been rough. That's part of the reason I stopped by—to check on you."

"Did you check on James, too?"

"Are you kidding?" Eddie said. "That kid came bursting out of the school building like it was the best day of his life. He's eating all this up. But you—you're more sensitive, so you're the one I was worried about. I know what that's like. I was a sensitive kid, too."

"It's just hard," Randy said, "having everybody thinking you're a liar."

"Well, I know you're not a liar," Eddie said. "And probably there are a lot of people in this town who don't think you're a liar, either. But it's easier for them to tell themselves you're lying because deep down, they're scared you're telling the truth."

It was the first thing anybody had said all day that made Randy feel a little better.

"Now, if you don't mind," Eddie said, "when we get close to your place, I'll just drop you at the head of the hollow. I don't want your momma and daddy to see my car. I figure I'm not exactly their favorite person right now."

Momma looked frazzled. Her hair was coming out of its bun, and her eyes had a wild, panicked quality. "The phone has been ringing off the hook all day," she said. "People who haven't so much as said hello to me in the grocery store in ten years all want to talk to me about you and the monster. And then there was some peculiar man from New Mexico who wanted to talk about aliens." She pushed a loose tendril of hair behind her ear. "I haven't been able to get a thing done around the house for talking to people."

"I'm sorry people are bothering you, Momma," Randy said. "This story has taken on a life of its own."

"It's taken over *our lives* is a better way of putting it," Daddy said. "Tell him about the magazine that called."

Momma walked over near the phone and picked up a slip of paper. "Yeah, it was a reporter from *Amazing But True* magazine. They want to pay you five hundred dollars for your story."

Randy's jaw dropped. He had never even seen that kind of money before. "Five hundred dollars? Are you kidding?"

"That's what the feller said." She set the slip of paper back down. "Me and your daddy having a little disagreement about it."

"Yeah," Daddy said. "Doc Carter says I've got to stay in the cast for four more weeks. Five hundred dollars would hold us a good long time till I'm able to work again."

"It would," Randy said. He felt a flicker of hope. Had his dad come around to believing that the monster was real? "Does that mean you believe in the monster now, Daddy?"

Daddy laughed. "No, but I sure do believe in getting five hundred dollars!"

Momma shook her head. "I don't want any money coming into this house that ain't earned honestly."

"It would be honest, Momma," Randy said. "I'm not lying about the monster."

Momma looked like she might cry. "I know you

believe it's real, honey. I'd probably be less worried if I thought you'd just cooked up a fib. I don't want nobody taking advantage of you because of what you thought you saw. Besides, what kind of way is that to make money, by telling a story?"

"Seems to me," Daddy said, "if they're willing to pay five hundred dollars for some crazy story, it's us who's taking advantage of them!"

Tension hung in the air all evening. When they sat down to eat their beans and corn bread and fried taters, nobody talked but Cindy, who prattled on about what she would name a horse if she had one. Momma and Daddy sat and listened to the radio like they did every night, Momma with her sewing and Daddy with his whittling. But the tension was still there, like an invisible glass wall that separated them from one another.

Randy lay in bed listening to his sister's soft snores, but he couldn't sleep. He had never meant to cause problems in his family. He had never meant to put himself in the position of being picked on mercilessly at school. He had always been taught that good things happened to you when you told the truth. But what if you told the truth and the people you were closest to didn't believe you?

From outside, there was a low humming sound that grew louder and louder. Green light streamed in through the bedroom window.

Randy sat bolt upright. "It's here."

"What's here?" Cindy said from the other side of the curtain.

"The monster. It's outside." Randy's heart was racing.

"I want to see."

Randy was tempted to tell her to stay inside, but he knew Cindy was stubborn and fearless, and there was no time to argue.

Barefoot and in his pajamas, Randy ran to the front door and went out on the front porch with Cindy right behind him. Nothing could have prepared him for what he saw when he looked at the sky.

A huge disk, bigger than his house, bigger than any building he had ever seen, was suspended in the air, producing the low humming sound he had heard from inside. The disk gave off the now-familiar green glow, but it was also illuminated with hundreds of lights making it shine like the world's largest Christmas tree.

"Wow." Cindy breathed.

Cindy grabbed Randy's hand, something she hadn't done since she was much littler. Speechless and in shock, Randy was grateful for the human contact.

At the bottom of the disk, a panel slid open. A

hooded green figure with glowing red eyes emerged from the opening. It hovered just below the floating disk, casting its eerie green glow over the house, the yard, the barn, the chicken coop. Even Bill's family's house was awash in the strange green light.

"What in the Sam Hill?" a voice behind Randy said.

Randy turned around to see Momma and Daddy standing behind him in their nightclothes, eyes wide, mouths agape.

Randy felt a sudden surge of fear that the people he loved might be in danger. He let go of his sister's hand and stepped down off the porch. "So you decided to come find me, did you?" he hollered up at the creature. "Listen, you can do what you want to me, but don't hurt my family, okay?"

The creature just floated silently.

"I'll give you what you want!" Randy yelled. "Take whatever you want as long as you don't hurt my family." Tears were welling in Randy's eyes. "Just take what you want and then go back where you came from!"

The creature turned and faced the chicken coop. It raised one cloaked arm. One of the hens, Anne Francis, floated out of the chicken coop, still asleep with her head tucked under her wing. She floated over, then upward toward the flying disk and disappeared into its opening. One by one, each chicken floated from the coop and into the open door of the flying disk. Only

Godzilla the rooster was awake during the process and seemed confused about how, without using his wings, he could fly to such un-chicken-like heights.

"What do you reckon it's gonna do with all them chickens?" Momma whispered.

"Who knows?" Daddy whispered back. "Eat them? Marry them?"

"Okay," Randy said, feeling suddenly sad about the loss of his beloved girls. "You wanted the chickens. Was that all?"

The figure turned so it was facing Bill's family's house. It was only now that Randy saw Bill standing on his porch in his pajamas. Randy wondered if Bill still thought the creature was a communist hoax.

And then it happened.

Bill was framed in the same green glow the chickens had been and was lifted off his feet. He floated slowly through the air, arms flailing, feet kicking, yelling, "No! No! Put me down!"

"Don't take my friend!" Randy yelled, but Bill's wriggling form disappeared into the door of the spacecraft.

"I'm calling the police," Momma said, running inside the house.

That was going to be an interesting phone call, Randy thought. He was sure he'd soon be lifted into the strange vessel, and the thought filled him with terror but also a burning curiosity.

But when the creature turned back to face him, it only nodded, then rose back up until it, too, disappeared inside the disk. The disk's humming sound grew louder, and it rose up, up, up into the sky until only darkness remained.

Randy couldn't speak. He couldn't process what had happened to Bill, to the chickens. He turned around to see his father leaning on his crutches, staring up at the now-empty sky.

"Do you believe me now?" Randy asked.

CHAPTER 12
THIRTY-TWO YEARS LATER
1988

"Y ou're Randy Siler, aren't you? *The* Randy Siler?"
The bearded young man's eyes were shining with
excitement. He held out his hand for Randy to shake.

"That's me," Randy said, shaking the man's hand.
"Where did you folks come from?"

The young man looked over at the young woman
who was standing slightly behind him. She was smiling politely, but didn't seem to be nearly as excited as
he was.

"We came all the way from Portland, Oregon. We
wanted to do some hiking on the Appalachian Trail."
The young man pronounced it *Apple-layshun*, like all

outsiders did. "But mainly we were looking for an excuse to visit the Mountain Monster Museum."

"Well, I'm glad you found one," Randy said. He took out a pushpin from a plastic box he kept near the cash register. "I've got a big map of the United States on the wall over there. Why don't you stick a pushpin into Portland, Oregon, on it? I like to keep track of where all our guests come from."

"Sure," the young man said, accepting the pushpin.

"Y'all look around and stay as long as you like," Randy said. "And let me know if you have any questions about the exhibits. Bill's around here somewhere. I'm sure he'll be happy to say howdy to you."

The young man's eyes grew wide. "Bill? Really? Cool!"

As the couple walked over to the map, the young man explained to his companion, "Bill was the other kid on the camping trip when the monster showed up the first time. Later the monster abducted him. There was a third kid, named James, who saw the monster at a later sighting, but he moved away from Green Mountain after living here only a year."

The girl nodded. Randy felt sorry for her. She clearly wasn't interested in any of this stuff.

Fifteen years ago, when Randy started talking about opening a museum downtown, people said he was crazy. Except for the city café, the drugstore, and a few offices, downtown Green Mountain was dead. Nobody went there. But Randy had spent a lot of time when he was younger having people say he was crazy when he knew he was right. He took a gamble on the chance that he might be right this time, too.

The museum had started small in the empty space that had been the hardware store, but over the years it had expanded to take up the space once held by the dime store and the flower shop. The museum displayed all the newspaper clippings about the monster and a gallery of artists' renderings of the monster and its spaceship. Guests could have their pictures taken with a life-size replica of the monster Randy had commissioned from a local artist. The monster was mounted so it seemed to hover above the floor, and its eyes were shining red lights. A green light bulb on the ceiling created the effect of an eerie glow.

And then there was the gift shop where guests could buy Green Mountain Monster T-shirts, key chains, and plush toy monsters that Randy's elderly momma sewed by the dozen. They could also purchase copies of Randy's self-published book, *The Monster and Me*.

But Randy didn't fool himself. He knew the biggest reason people came to the museum was because of its living attraction.

When Bill had been lifted into the monster's space-craft, Randy had thought he'd never see Bill again. But three days later, he found Bill staggering through the cow pasture, hungry, thirsty, and confused.

After Randy walked Bill back to his house for a tearful reunion with his parents, Bill had drunk a big glass of water and eaten two ham biscuits before he would speak of his adventure. He said there were other creatures on the ship who looked just like the one they had seen in the woods, which made Randy wonder if he had been seeing a different creature at each sighting. Bill said the aliens hadn't been cruel to him. They had kept him in a clear tank, like an aquarium but without water. They observed him closely, even though he wasn't really doing anything. Each day they gave him a cup of water and a raw egg from the chickens. He didn't have the language to communicate with them that he needed more to eat and drink and that eggs were supposed to be cooked.

Bill said it was funny. The creatures had kept him confined in a tank, but they let the chickens roam free all over the spaceship and scattered cracked corn for them on the spaceship's floor. When the aliens looked at the chickens, they vibrated and made an odd little thrumming sound. After a while, Bill decided this sound must be laughter.

The aliens seemed to be fascinated by Earth and its creatures, and Bill said that they had visited Earth for research purposes and had taken samples of its creatures to study them. But were they studying Earth so they could take it over, or just so they could understand it? This was the question Randy always asked, and Bill was either unable or unwilling to answer it.

Though Randy never said it aloud, he always found it interesting that the aliens had kept the chickens but had sent Bill back.

Lots of people said Bill wasn't the same once he came back, and it was true. He was distracted and dreamy in school and often seemed faraway, like he had left a part of himself on the spaceship. However, in many ways he was a better friend. He apologized to Randy for calling him a chicken and a communist and saying the monster wasn't real. Their friendship resumed and hadn't stopped since.

By the time Randy was ready to open the museum, Bill had been fired from a series of jobs and was down on his luck and unable to pay for even his small rented room. Randy gave Bill the official title of museum custodian, but Randy had really hired him to be a living artifact more than anything else. He knew people would want to hear Bill tell his story.

Randy was unpacking a new box of T-shirts for the gift shop when Bill walked into the front room. "I was just talking to them people from . . . was it Idaho?" Bill had some laugh lines around his eyes and mouth, but he was still boyish looking.

"Oregon," Randy said, placing a stack of folded T-shirts on a shelf.

"Yeah, that was it," Bill said. "That feller sure was interested in me. He asked me everything but what I had for breakfast. Speaking of that, I was gonna run next door for a cup of coffee. You want anything?"

"No, thanks. I'm good," Randy said.

"You don't want a Monster Burger?"

Randy smiled. "I believe I'll pass." Cashing in on the success of the museum, the city café had a sign outside announcing itself as HOME OF THE MONSTER BURGER.

As Bill left, a family of four came in. Randy greeted them and sold them their tickets.

The little boy, who seemed to be about four, looked up at Randy and said, "Is this gonna be scary?"

"No, not at all," Randy said, smiling down at him. "It's fun."

At 6 p.m., Randy hung the CLOSED sign on the door of the museum like he always did. Bill's mop bucket was propping open the door of the men's restroom. Cleaning the restrooms was the last thing he did every day. Randy hollered into the open door. "You want the usual, buddy?"

"You know I do," Bill called back. "Thanks, buddy!"

Randy went outside and got into the very comfortable car the monster museum had made possible for him. He drove away from town and toward the interstate exit and pulled into the drive-thru at the Chicken Bucket.

"Thank you for choosing the Chicken Bucket. May I take your order?" the familiar voice on the intercom asked.

"Yes, you may, Melissa," Randy said.

There was laughter over the intercom. "Oh, hi, Mr. Siler. Was you wanting a three-piece dark meal for your friend?"

"Yes, please. Two legs and a thigh." He made the same order at the same time every day. It was important to keep Bill happy. Fortunately, it didn't take much. Buying a daily box of chicken wasn't like making a blood sacrifice or anything, and it was enough to pacify Bill and keep things running smoothly.

Randy took the food and drove back to the museum. By the time he got there, both of the restroom doors were shut, which meant that Bill had finished his cleaning. Randy walked through the museum all the way to the back to the door marked *Private*. He knocked.

"Just a minute," Bill's voice called.

When Randy had hired Bill all those years ago, part of the arrangement had been that Bill was welcome to live in the back room for free in exchange for keeping an eye on the place. Randy had thought this would be temporary, until Bill had saved up enough money for an apartment or house. But Bill had stayed in the back room for over a decade now. It was cozy, he said.

Bill answered the door in his undershirt and boxer shorts. "Sorry," he said with a sheepish grin. "I'm changing. You can come on in, though."

"Thanks," Randy said, closing the door and locking it. "By the end of the day, I'm sure you're glad to take all that off."

"I sure am," Bill said. He reached around to the back of his head to the little button that was hidden by his hair. When he touched it, the flesh on his head and face split into two perfectly symmetrical halves. Bill grabbed the two segments and pulled them down to neck level, then shoulder level, then chest level. Randy had witnessed this many times, but it never ceased to amaze him to see Bill peel himself like a banana.

As the human skin fell away, the room filled with a green glow. The figure, also green, hovered just above the human skin that now lay crumpled on the floor like an old raincoat. With its glowing red eyes, it stared at the box of fried chicken Randy held out as an offering.

CHAPTER 1

Today she felt like the 1940s, Maisie decided. Standing in front of her closet full of vintage dresses, she selected a red-and-white polka-dotted number with padded shoulders and a sweetheart neckline. It looked like the kind of dress a girl in the '40s might have worn to a dance where she would jitterbug the night away with a handsome soldier to the brassy sounds of a big band.

She put on the dotted dress and a pair of peep-toed slingback pumps, which hurt her feet but looked great. She sat down at her vanity to work on her hair and makeup. Maisie kept her chestnut-brown hair a little longer than shoulder length so she could have the maximum versatility of style. Today she pulled her hair into a ponytail and stuffed it inside a snood, a fancy hairnet that women in the '40s used to keep their hair out of the way.

And now it was time for the forties face. Maisie smoothed on a light foundation, then highlighted her eyebrows with a brow pencil. She applied liquid rouge using the "three-dot" method she had learned from an online makeup tutorial, then applied mascara to her upper lashes only. She finished with bright red lipstick that matched her dress. The redder, the better.

Maisie stood in front of her full-length mirror and put on a pair of vintage clip-on earrings that pinched her earlobes like vises. She looked herself over. "Not bad," she said. Sure, there were more details she could have worked on—some seamed stockings would have been nice if she'd had them—but overall, for a school day, it was a solid look.

Maisie walked down the hall to the kitchen, her shoes clip-clopping on the hardwood floor.

Her dad was sitting at the kitchen table with his toast and coffee. His dull brown hair was cut in a standard middle-aged white guy haircut, and he was wearing the polo shirt and khakis he always wore to work. He looked like such a dad. "Say, is that Rosie the Riveter that I spy?" he asked.

Maisie resisted the urge to roll her eyes. She knew her dad meant well, even if he said the cheesiest things. "Yes, but Rosie's going to a dance," she said, spinning around so her dress flared. She had another outfit that was truly Rosie the Riveter, a pair of blue coveralls and a red head scarf that made her look like she was ready for a long day at the munitions factory. But hey, at least her dad was in the right decade.

"You want a smoothie?" her mom asked.

"Yes, please," Maisie said. Her mom knew her well. She knew Maisie liked a light, nutritious breakfast she could drink through a straw. That way, she wouldn't muss up her lipstick.

Her mom dumped some sliced peaches, berries, and yogurt into the blender and pushed the button. Once the whirring noises stopped, she said, "I know I say this all the time, but I just don't see how you find the energy every day to make yourself look so different and special."

Maisie shrugged. "If everybody found the energy, the world would be a less-boring place."

"Well, it would *look* less boring, that's for sure," Mom said, pouring the contents of the blender into a glass. "But looks aren't everything."

Maisie thought her mom was naturally pretty, but it annoyed her that she took no pains with her appearance whatsoever. She wore the same kind of dress slacks and button-down blouse to her job at the credit union every day, and her idea of primping was brushing her hair and her teeth. "Well, that would at least be a start, wouldn't it?" Maisie said, taking the glass of pulverized fruit and sticking a straw in it.

"I'm just glad we don't live in a time when women *have* to get dressed up to go out of the house," Mom said, sitting down with her toast and coffee. "Like those pictures of your grandma where she had on a dress and high heels and a hat and little white gloves when she was just going out to the grocery store or something."

"I think G.G. looks very pretty in those pictures," Maisie said, being careful not to spill any of her smoothie.

"I do, too," Mom said. "But all that getup looks so uncomfortable. I don't think I ever would've left the house if I had to go to all that trouble."

"I'll take beauty over comfort any day," Maisie said.

Maisie wished she had been born in a different time. People in the 2020s padded around in their sneakers or flip-flops and track pants or pajama bottoms, even though they were out in public. It was like nobody could be bothered with getting dressed for the day. All the other decades had their own styles—the bobbed hair and fringed dresses of the 1920s, the ponytails and poodle skirts of the 1950s, even the long hair and love beads and bell-bottoms of the 1960s. But she was living in an era with no style, no sense of what was beautiful or good. Nothing mattered to people but convenience and comfort.

It wasn't just the way people looked. It was how they lived their lives, too. The food they ate was low-quality, just high-speed junk grabbed from a drive-thru window or thrown into a microwave. Communication was also fast and cheap, typed out in misspelled text messages or short posts on social media. Maisie longed for a time when people valued face-to-face conversation.

She only owned a cell phone because her parents made her carry one in case of emergency. She hated seeing it inside her vintage purse. It totally ruined the effect, like when a takeout paper coffee cup accidentally ends up in a frame of a movie set in another era.

After Maisie finished her smoothie, she grabbed her backpack—another practical item that annoyed her because it interfered with the historical authenticity of her outfit—and walked to school. She tried to walk in a sort of jaunty, sassy 1940s style, the way Barbara Stanwyck did in a comedy she'd seen on the classic movie channel. She also tried not to walk like her shoes were hurting her feet, which they were.

Northwest High School, where Maisie was a sophomore, was an abomination of modern institutional architecture. It was basically a series of rectangular boxes made of ugly brown brick. It looked like something a toddler would build out of blocks.

Maisie sighed as she entered the ugly building. No matter how good she felt when she woke up in the morning and started putting her look together, once she was in school, she felt drained of all energy. The environment was just so uninspiring.

As she trudged down the hall, some normie girl in yoga pants and a Northwest High Panthers T-shirt said, "Every day is Halloween for you, isn't it?"

"Wow, that's so original. I've never heard that one before," Maisie said, not slowing her pace. Every day at school she heard some variation on this theme. Boring people were so dull they couldn't even insult you in an interesting way.

That being said, Halloween was her favorite holiday, so she didn't really take the girl's words as that much of an insult.

When she entered homeroom, she walked past the boring kids in their jeans and sweatpants and stupid, trendy haircuts and sat in the back corner near a couple of Goths. With their bright hair dye and black clothing, their style was different than Maisie's, but at least they were trying for *something*.

As soon as Maisie sat down, she saw Abby come into the room. Abby spotted her right away, and her lips spread in a braces-filled smile. She gave Maisie a happy little wave and made a beeline for the seat next to hers. Abby seemed so excited to be in Maisie's presence. It was like they hadn't seen each other in months when really it had been just yesterday.

"Oh my gosh, you look so pretty!" Abby gushed, sitting down next to Maisie. "That's the dress you ordered from that retro store online, right?"

"Uh-huh," Maisie said. It was funny, but she always seemed to fall into this pattern with Abby. The more enthusiastic Abby was, the flatter Maisie's tone became. Maisie wasn't sure why she did this. It was terrible to say, but sometimes she felt overwhelmed by Abby's niceness.

"I should get an after-school job, too, so I can save up to buy some new clothes. I really would like to look better," Abby said. "But band practice takes so much time, and I have to play at all the games, so it's hard to schedule work hours."

Maisie wondered what kind of new clothes Abby would buy. She certainly didn't work very hard on her look. She still wore her hair in the same box braids she'd had in middle school. They looked cool, but why not try something new? Today Abby was wearing jeans and a T-shirt printed with a cartoon cat eating a taco that said TACO CAT SPELLED BACKWARD IS STILL TACO CAT, along with jeans and a pair of Keds. The thing was, with her blemish-free dark complexion and willowy build, Abby was a natural beauty. She just didn't do anything to enhance what nature had given her. "You don't have to have that much money to get some new looks," Maisie said. "You could always go thrifting."

Abby's big brown eyes shone with excitement. "Hey, maybe you could take me thrifting one day? I mean, I could use your expertise. I wouldn't know where to go or what to buy."

"Sure," Maisie said.

It wasn't that Maisie didn't like Abby. Abby was her only real friend at Northwest High, so if she didn't like Abby, she'd be totally alone. But Abby seemed to like Maisie so much—and *admire* her so much—that she gave the impression that she was desperate for Maisie's friendship and approval. Maisie wished Abby didn't try so hard. And while Maisie would never say it out loud, in her heart, she wished for another kind of friend. Not instead of Abby, but in addition to Abby. A friend who was glamorous and sophisticated, someone who she could admire and learn from. But there was no chance of meeting anybody like that in this place. Not here and not now.

CHAPTER 2

Saturday was Maisie's favorite. It was Flea Market Day.

Her Saturday morning ritual never varied. She woke up at eight, so she'd have plenty of time to get ready and arrive exactly when the flea market opened at ten. Her look for Flea Market Day always took careful consideration. She wanted to give off the retro-cool vibe, but she also needed to be comfortable enough for a few hours of browsing, so slingback pumps just weren't happening.

Today she decided to go for a 1950s casual teen look. She put on a pair of vintage jeans, which she rolled up just under her knees, and a loose-fitting white button-down shirt, which she left untucked. She put on bobby socks and comfy saddle oxfords. She finished her look by tying a pink chiffon scarf around her neck and putting her hair in a high ponytail. She powdered her nose, put on a little lipstick, and stuffed her available money in a small pink drawstring purse that matched her scarf.

She headed out the door without telling her parents where she was going. Since it was Saturday, they would know where she was.

The walk to the flea market took twenty minutes. On her way, she always stopped at Java Jive, the café where she worked a couple of afternoons a week, for a free coffee. Depending on who was working on Saturday morning, she could sometimes score a free scone as well.

She opened the café's door, and the inviting smell of coffee hit her. The whole place was inviting, really. There were tables and chairs for guests who wanted to eat or work and soft purple couches for those who wanted to lounge. The exposed brick walls were always hung with paintings by local artists, and jazz played softly through the speakers. Sean was behind the counter, which meant it was definitely a scone day. Sean was a freshman at Southeast High across town, and Maisie was pretty sure he had a crush on her. He certainly had a tendency to struggle for words and drop things when she was around.

"Oh, hi, Maisie!" Sean said. He was skinny and shorter than Maisie, one of those unfortunate boys who's still waiting for his growth spurt even though he's in high school.

"Hey, Sean," Maisie said.

"Headed to the flea market?" he asked. He was already starting Maisie's regular order, a mocha with whipped cream and an extra pump of chocolate.

"Yeah."

"I might head over there myself after I get off at one," Sean said. "My friend told me there was a guy selling Magic cards last week. He said they were pretty overpriced, though."

Maisie didn't respond. Sean was one of those guys who was super into nerdy card games. Sometimes his friends came into the café and played there. They'd get all excited and yell about spells and wizards and stuff.

"Hey, uh . . ." Sean looked at Maisie, then blushed and looked away. "How about a lemon-blueberry scone on the house?"

"Sure, thanks," Maisie said.

"Yeah, I'm probably not supposed to be giving away the merchandise, but they can always take it out of my paycheck," he said, handing her the scone in a napkin and a to-go cup of coffee. "Careful, the coffee's hot."

She knew the coffee was hot. She worked there, too. "Thanks," she said, trying not to let her annoyance show.

"Hey, uh . . ." Sean said again, "maybe I'll see you at the flea market later?"

"Could be," Maisie said. She made a mental note to be sure to be done with the flea market by 1 p.m. She didn't want Sean tagging along behind her, tripping over his words and his own feet.

The Village Antique and Flea Market was an assault on the senses. The smell of the fried food at the concession stand always hit Maisie first when she walked through the door. People of all ages, from grandmas in tracksuits to sticky-faced toddlers, crowded the narrow passageways between booths selling knockoff versions of name-brand sneakers and purses, T-shirts, and video games. A Mennonite family who owned an orchard sold fresh apples, jugs of apple cider, and cinnamony cider doughnuts. A scrawny man with a mullet presided over a booth selling both lethal-looking knives and bootleg DVDs. At the next booth was an old man in overalls with cages full of squawking live chickens for sale. You had to know where to go to find the real treasures. Most of the antique and vintage dealers were in Hall D, so Maisie headed in that direction.

She walked past booths selling antique furniture and vintage dishware. Sometimes she liked to look at these things and imagine how she would decorate her house when she grew up. Would she have the whole house themed to a certain era, or would she mix it up? She might come by and look at furniture and dishes and daydream a little later, but for now she decided to see if there was anyone selling vintage clothes or accessories.

Most of the vendors were Saturday regulars, just like she was. But the very last booth on the left was a new one.

The first thing she noticed was not the contents of the booth but the woman who was staffing it. Petite, both short and small-boned, she was wearing a floor-length black velvet gown. The gown had long sleeves and a high lace collar decorated with a shiny, black jet brooch. The bodice of the gown fit tight around the woman's torso, and her waist seemed impossibly tiny.

Maisie mentally reviewed her knowledge of Victorian fashion. A corset. To make her waist look so tiny, the woman must be wearing a corset. Maisie had to admit she was impressed. Wearing one of those things must have been miserable. This was a woman who was totally committed to her look.

She was even wearing high-button shoes, the kind that would have to be put on with a buttonhook. Her hair was piled onto her head in an elaborate updo. This ensemble was not an example of steampunk or even the neo-Victorian look, where nineteenth century–inspired bits and pieces were often combined with more modern items. This look was authentic, as if the woman had stepped from the pages of a Victorian ladies' magazine.

Stricken shy, Maisie cautiously approached the booth. Taking her eyes off the woman for a moment, she took in the glass cases of vintage jewelry. A narrow window overhead let in a stream of light that made the brooches, bracelets, and necklaces sparkle like stars. Between the woman and the booth, Maisie felt overwhelmed by beauty, a resource that she felt was sadly scarce in the cold, bland, modern world.

"Good morning, dear," the woman said. Her voice was rich and warm, like the cup of coffee Maisie had just drunk. It was hard to figure the woman's age. She was definitely older than college age but probably younger than Maisie's mom. Whatever her age, she was lovely. Her brown eyes were framed in dark lashes and deep set, and her cheekbones were high and well defined.

"Hello," Maisie said, shocked by how timid she felt.

"Please come in and look around," the woman said, gesturing at the glittering cases around her. "You strike me as a young woman with discerning taste."

"Thank you." Maisie was flattered by the compliment. However, even if she did have discerning taste, she was pretty sure she didn't have the kind of money she needed to buy antique jewelry of this quality. "I may just browse a little," she said, sounding apologetic.

"Please," the woman said. "Enjoy looking. Fine jewelry is art, and this is my little museum." She smiled. "But isn't it lovely that it's art you can wear?"

Maisie smiled back and looked in the cases. She had never seen such high-quality antique accessories. One case was devoted entirely to cameo brooches and another to ornate rings with large stone settings, one of which had a green jewel framed by golden rams' heads on either side. A small handwritten sign under this collection labeled them POISON RINGS. Maisie remembered an old movie she had seen in which a lady had opened a secret compartment in her ring and discreetly dispensed some hidden arsenic into her unfaithful husband's drink. Maisie wondered if any of these rings had been used to kill people. A little spooked, she moved on to the next case, which contained sparkling, black jet mourning jewelry.

"I am fond of the mourning jewelry myself," the woman said, touching the black brooch she wore at her throat. "Do you see that necklace? The one with what looks like a small rope woven among the beads?"

Maisie nodded.

"The rope is actually a braided clipping from the departed's hair," the woman said with a wistful smile. "It was customary to snip off a lock of the hair of the deceased and incorporate it into mourning jewelry. As a remembrance."

"I think I read about that somewhere," Maisie said. She looked at the light brown tendril wrapped around the shining beads and wondered who it had belonged to. It was too long to have belonged to a man of that era. A woman? A child? She was fascinated but also uneasy; she wasn't sure she could bring herself to wear a piece of jewelry woven with the hair of a long-dead stranger, though she imagined one of the Goth kids at school might.

Maisie moved on to the next case. In it, lying on a square of dark purple velvet, was a piece of jewelry unlike anything Maisie had ever seen before. It was a large silver brooch with hanging chains from which dangled a miniature pincushion, a tiny pair of scissors, a thimble, and a buttonhook. "What's this?" Maisie asked.

"Oh, you have a good eye for jewelry," the woman said. "That is a chatelaine. It's an interestingly functional piece of jewelry. Ladies used to wear chatelaines to hold their necessities because their clothing lacked pockets. Mistresses of great houses wore them to hold their keys; other ladies—like the lady who owned this one—used them for tiny sewing kits."

Maisie loved how the piece was beautiful but also served a practical purpose. Even the word for it— *chatelaine*—was beautiful. She found herself wanting it desperately, maybe more than she had ever wanted any vintage item. She couldn't explain why she longed for it, but the desire felt physical, like the chatelaine was food or water instead of a decorative object. "How much?" she asked. Even as the words came out of her mouth, she felt drained of hope. She knew it would cost more than she could afford.

"Hmm . . ." the woman said, running her hand over the glass case containing the chatelaine. "As I said, I can tell you have a good eye and that you truly appreciate the piece. I wouldn't sell this piece to just anyone. So . . . for you . . . fifty dollars?"

It was a lot less than Maisie had expected. She had just gotten paid for her part-time job at Java Jive, and she had seventy dollars in her purse. "Okay," she said, smiling. She could scarcely believe her good luck. "I'll take it."

"Wonderful," the woman said, smiling back at Maisie. "Let me wrap it up for you. A special piece deserves a beautiful package. And so does a special girl."

Maisie felt her face heat up. She was flattered that this woman who was such a pinnacle of style saw something in her that was worthy of admiration. She watched as the woman carefully lifted the chatelaine from its glass case, wrapped it in crimson tissue paper, and placed it in a purple-and-gold box. "For you," she said.

Maisie placed her money in the woman's hand and accepted the beautiful box.

CHAPTER 3

Ideally, Maisie would wear the chatelaine with a Victorian gown, but there was no way she had the money to afford one of those right now, even a more reasonably priced reproduction. So she settled on wearing the chatelaine on her simplest black vintage dress, the one her mom called the Audrey Hepburn dress because of the actress's famous look.

Audrey Hepburn was onto something. The chatelaine showed itself beautifully on a simple black background, and when Maisie wore it to school, she felt people's admiring eyes on it.

Abby noticed it as soon as she walked into homeroom. "Okay, that's new," she said, sitting down next to Maisie. "I mean," she said smiling, "it's old, but it's new."

"Yes, it's new to me," Maisie said. "I got it for a steal at the flea market on Saturday."

Abby reached out to touch the brooch. "It's stunning. What is it?"

"It's called a chatelaine."

"Oh, that's French," Abby said. Abby's mom was from Cameroon, so she had grown up speaking French. Abby wasn't fluent, but she knew enough that she was far and away the best student in French I.

"Yes," Maisie said. "I bet you can pronounce it better than I can."

"Chatelaine," Abby said with a perfect accent.

"Yep," Maisie said, laughing.

A couple of the Goth kids approached Maisie's desk.

"Hey, we were just looking at that piece of jewelry," the purple-haired girl said.

"Yeah, what is it?" the blue-haired boy asked.

"C'est une chatelaine," Abby said.

Maisie gave a mini-lecture on what a chatelaine was, and the Goth kids listened attentively.

"It's cool," Purple Hair Girl said. "Especially the scissors."

Throughout the school day, more and more people noticed the chatelaine. At lunch, a group of theater kids crowded around Maisie to admire it. Even her history teacher seemed fascinated by it, especially when Maisie told her about the purpose chatelaines had served for Victorian ladies. When Maisie came home from school after wearing the chatelaine for the first time, she felt like it was one of the best days she could remember.

That night, after she finished her homework, Maisie lay on her bed, still wearing the black dress and chatelaine, and flipped through her favorite book, *Fashion Through the Decades*, looking for inspiration for the kind of Victorian outfit she would put together when she could afford one. Maybe, when she went back to the flea market on Saturday, she could ask the woman at the jewelry booth where she had found her clothing.

But Maisie was tired. As she turned the pages, her eyes grew heavy, and soon she was curled up on top of the covers asleep, her arms around her book as if it were a teddy bear.

Click, click, click. Maisie's high-button boots hit the cobblestone streets as she walked through the neighborhood of grand houses decked out with towers and wraparound porches and gingerbread trim. Maisie sensed that she was standing up straighter than usual and that walking took a strange amount of effort. Looking down, she saw that the challenge came from the long, pearl-gray skirt she was wearing, seemingly with a thick petticoat underneath it. With each step, she kicked forward the heavy fabric. The reason for her posture became clear when she put her hand on her stomach and felt the rigid frame of a corset holding her torso in place. It felt like her soft flesh had been crammed into the stiff scaffolding of a building. It wasn't underwear; it was architecture.

Maisie was confused about where she was and how she was dressed, though, she was a little reassured when she looked down at her bodice and saw the familiar chatelaine pinned there.

Wait, I'm dreaming, aren't I? Maisie thought, as she often did in her dreams. She had learned in psychology class that this kind of lucid dreaming was rare, but it wasn't rare for her. Usually there was a moment where she told herself she was dreaming, felt comforted, and then just let the action unfold like a movie playing in her head. *I'm dreaming, and it's a Victorian dream, which makes perfect sense since I was looking at Victorian fashion before I fell asleep. Okay, so I should just go with it.*

Feeling relieved that none of her surroundings were real, Maisie continued down the stone street. She noticed she was carrying a small card in one hand that read *1202 Bluebell Lane, four o'clock, May 3, 1885.* She wondered if that was the "current" date in this dream. A bell from a nearby church tower tolled four times. When she reached a corner, she looked up at the street sign and saw she was already on Bluebell Lane. Suddenly, she realized where she was—in an old section of town where in present day, some of these old Victorian homes still stood, though most of them had been divided up into cheap apartments for college students.

The house at 1202 Bluebell Lane was robin's egg blue with cream-colored gingerbread trim. On the second story, a tower that reminded Maisie of "Rapunzel" overlooked the well-tended flowerbeds of pansies and petunias in the yard. Maisie didn't know why she was here or whom she was meeting, but since the logic of the dream was telling her this was the place to be, she walked up the steps to the porch, holding her long skirt so as not to trip over it, and used the lion's head–shaped knocker on the front door.

In just a moment, the door opened. A girl with striking red curls, not much older than Maisie, wearing an apron over a plain white blouse and long dark skirt, said, "Good afternoon. Please come in. Miss Violet is expecting you."

Violet, Maisie told herself. *The person I'm meeting is named Violet.* "Thank you," Maisie said, following the maid into the opulent living room. The operative word to describe the decor was *busy*. Flocked floral wallpaper competed with the paisley print of the sofa and the elaborate patterns of the Oriental rugs. It was a riot of different colors. The walls were hung with mirrors and assorted paintings, still lifes of fruits and flowers, and a portrait of a sad-eyed spaniel, and little porcelain figurines of dairy maids and ladies in ball gowns and playful kittens cluttered the coffee table and the mantel. Clearly whoever lived here did not follow the philosophy that less is more.

Maisie was so fascinated by her surroundings that at first she didn't notice the young woman coming toward her. "Maisie!" she called, sounding genuinely happy to see her.

"Violet!" Maisie said, hoping she was guessing right.

The girl who was approaching Maisie with open arms was startlingly pretty. Her blonde hair, which had a lot of natural curl, was piled on top of her head, and her very blue eyes matched her long, lace-trimmed dress. Maisie guessed that she was probably around seventeen.

The girl hugged Maisie, kissed her cheek, and then stood holding her hands and gazing at her, smiling. "How well you look!" she said. "But aren't you naughty, coming all this way by yourself without a chaperone?"

"I, uh—" Maisie had no idea what to say. "Yeah, I guess I'm pretty naughty," she finally managed.

"I know you think you're too old for a governess,

but your papa definitely disagrees with you," Violet said. "Maybe if your poor mama were still with you, he would think differently, but I'm sure he feels that with her gone, you need a feminine influence."

Maisie just nodded. She was overwhelmed by the amount of information that was getting thrown at her. It was hard to keep up. In the grand scheme of things, it probably didn't matter what she said or did because it was only a dream. Still, it was an interesting dream, and she wanted to play along.

"Please sit down," Violet said. "You must be exhausted from your long walk here." She looked over at the maid, who had been standing unobtrusively in the corner. "Maggie, you may bring in the coffee."

"Yes, ma'am." The maid disappeared into what Maisie assumed was the kitchen.

"Does embroidery make your fingers sore?" Violet asked, looking down at her fingertips.

"What?" Maisie asked. It was a natural response to a confusing question, but she reminded herself it wasn't natural for a girl in 1885. "I mean, I beg your pardon?"

"I was working on my embroidery before you arrived, and it always makes my fingertips terribly sore, like someone has been pinching them."

"Oh," Maisie said, trying to think of something to add to the conversation.

Fortunately, she was rescued by Maggie returning

with a cart laid out with coffee things, a fancy silver coffee pot and two dainty floral-painted china cups resting on gold-rimmed saucers. There was a sugar bowl, too, and a little pitcher for cream. It made Maisie think of a real version of a tea set a little girl would use for a tea party with her dolls and teddy bear.

"How do you like your coffee, Miss?" Maggie asked.

How do I like it? Maisie wondered. She was usually a mocha-with-an-extra-pump-of-chocolate girl, but she figured that was way out of Maggie's skill set. "Just with a splash of cream, please."

Maggie poured the steaming coffee, then a thin stream of cream, which she stirred with a tiny silver spoon before handing the cup to Maisie. "Thank you," Maisie said. It felt weird to be waited on, not in a café or restaurant, but in somebody's house.

Maggie poured Violet a cup of coffee with milk and sugar and then reached onto a lower shelf on the tea trolley and produced two plates, one of dainty cookies and another of small crustless sandwiches.

"Oh, Maggie, you do spoil us so!" Violet said, sipping her tea.

"Will that be all for now, Miss?" Maggie asked.

"Yes, Maggie. Thank you," Violet said.

Maisie had read books in which people had servants, but this was the closest she had ever come to witnessing it in person. How strange to have someone in your house whom you ordered around to do things for you.

"Do help yourself to sandwiches and cookies," Violet said, though she didn't seem to be taking any herself. "Maggie makes the most marvelous cucumber sandwiches. I don't know how she does it, but she slices the cucumbers as thin as paper."

Maisie took a sandwich and bit into it. She tasted the paper-thin cucumber, creamy butter, and soft white bread. *Wait,* Maisie thought. *Why am I able to taste food? When I eat in dreams, I never taste anything.* She took a sip of coffee. She felt its warmth in her mouth and tasted the bitterness and the smoothness of the cream. This was the most lifelike dream she had ever had.

"I'm sure this is all very simple compared to what you're used to in your house with your maid and your cook and your governess. We can only afford Maggie since Mama and Papa caught that terrible illness and passed away." She sipped her tea thoughtfully. "Say, I wonder if that's why you and I have become such fast friends. Do you think it's because we're both orphans?"

"Orphans?" Maisie said, nibbling a buttery cookie. She wasn't an orphan in real life, but maybe she was one in the story line of this dream. Which was strange. Morbid, even.

Violet smiled. "Well, you still have your father, of course. But really, anyone who has gone through the

139

terrible experience of losing even one parent counts as an orphan, don't you think?"

"Definitely," Maisie said. She certainly wasn't contributing much to this conversation. Fortunately, Violet seemed to be a talker, so maybe she didn't notice.

Violet set down her teacup and clapped her hands. "But this is a pleasant occasion. We shouldn't speak of such sad subjects. Tell me, are you excited about the tea dance on Saturday?"

"Very," Maisie said, since it seemed to be the right answer.

"I am, too!" Violet said. "I must show you the new gown I bought for the occasion. It's a lovely shade of . . . violet!" She giggled.

"Violet for Violet," Maisie said, trying to join in on what passed for hilarity in this setting.

"Exactly!" Violet said.

The front door opened with a loud creak. A young man wearing a top hat, a dark suit, and a cravat entered. He removed his hat and hung it on the coatrack near the door.

"Edwin!" Violet called to him, then turned to Maisie. "Maisie, I believe you are well acquainted with my brother."

"Of course," Maisie said, though she had never laid eyes on him. "Hello, Edwin." She was glad that Violet had said his name so that she could parrot it.

"Good afternoon, ladies," Edwin said, giving a slight bow. He had his sister's blond hair, but his was cut short with peculiar sideburns that grew down his cheeks. He also had an extremely well-groomed mustache that curled upward at the ends. It was hard for Maisie to determine how old he was—perhaps in his early twenties, though, everyone's elaborate dress and grooming made them look older than they were. Edwin was wearing a charcoal-gray waistcoat and trousers with a burgundy vest and matching ascot. If it were modern times, he would have looked like a member of a wedding party.

"Won't you join us for coffee, dear brother?" Violet asked.

Maisie couldn't explain why, but she didn't want Edwin to join them. Maybe it was because she and Violet were just getting to know each other, or maybe it was because there was something about Edwin that she immediately didn't like. You just had a feeling about some people. Whatever the reason, she hoped Edwin would decline Violet's offer.

Edwin smiled beneath his mustache. "With company this charming, how could I refuse?"

"Wonderful," Violet said. "I'll ring Maggie to bring you a cup and saucer." She picked up a bell that was sitting on the coffee table and shook it. *The sound was pretty obnoxious*, Maisie thought. She felt sorry for Maggie, who had been trained to respond to a bell like those dogs in the experiment Maisie had read about in her psychology class.

Maggie appeared almost immediately.

"Maggie, Edwin has decided to join us. Could you bring him a cup and a saucer and a plate, please?"

"Yes, Miss." Maggie scurried away.

Edwin asked for coffee with milk and four cubes of sugar, then loaded his plate with piles of the sandwiches and cookies.

"You must forgive my brother's appetite," Violet said. "He always eats ravenously."

"Mama always said I eat so much because I'm a growing boy," Edwin said, "but I'm not growing anymore. Though if Maggie keeps making these delicious cookies, I may very well grow fat!"

Violet giggled. "Well, there's nothing wrong with a little extra weight on a man. It means he's prosperous. A good provider."

Edwin smiled. There were cookie crumbs in his mustache. "Our father was a good provider, wasn't he, Violet? And I have to say he looked very, very prosperous."

Violet was smiling, but she said, "It's disrespectful to make fun of dear Papa, rest his soul. Maisie and I were just talking about the tea dance on Saturday."

"Ah, yes, the social event of the season!" Edwin said. "Maisie, I certainly hope you'll do me the honor of a dance."

"Well, I'm not much of a dancer," Maisie said. This statement was true in her real life, and she certainly didn't know anything about the kind of dancing Edwin and Violet would do. But maybe in this dream, she could dance. She had had dreams before in which she possessed abilities she didn't have in real life. Once she had dreamed that she could fly.

"Oh, Maisie, you're too modest," Violet said. "When we took dancing lessons, you were so much more graceful than I was."

"That wouldn't be difficult," Edwin said. "I adore you, dear sister, but you are quite clumsy." He looked at Maisie. His eyes were a startling light blue. "Perhaps you can let me be the judge of your dancing skills on Saturday night."

Before Maisie could answer, a loud buzzing sound filled her ears. She awoke to find herself in her room, still in her black Audrey Hepburn dress with the chatelaine pinned to it. She must have fallen asleep reading. Her eyes felt gritty, and she had drooled on her pillow. She turned off her alarm. It was 6:45 a.m. Time to get ready for school.

Maisie unpinned the chatelaine and took off her dress from the day before. She definitely needed a shower.

Standing under the jets of hot water, Maisie tried to piece together the dream. Usually, she didn't remember much about her dreams—just a few weird, disjointed images. But this dream had been so vivid that she could remember everything about it—the feel of the cobblestone streets beneath her high-button shoes, the weight of her long skirt, and the way the stays on her corset had dug into the skin around her ribs. She remembered the taste of the coffee and cucumber sandwiches, how Violet had looked and sounded, the strange combination of friendliness and formality in their conversation. She remembered Edwin, too—the crumbs in his mustache, the attempts at being charming, which had fallen flat in her opinion. Her recollection didn't feel like it was about a dream; it felt like a memory of something that had really happened.

CHAPTER 4

Maisie, today dressed in the short trousers and cap of a 1920s newsboy, walked up to Ms. Winters, her psychology teacher, after class was over.

Ms. Winters gave Maisie a friendly smile. She was an older lady who wore reading glasses that always slipped down her nose, and her hair was always twisted up in a bun that had a pencil stuck through it. Maisie always wondered if the pencil thing was just when she was at school or if it was something she did all the time. Did she go out to dinner with her husband with a pencil in her hair?

"Something I can help you with, Maisie?" Ms. Winters asked.

"Well, it's not for class or anything," Maisie said, feeling a little awkward suddenly. "But I'm interested in learning more about dreams. I had a really intense dream last night, and I can't stop thinking about it."

"Hmm," Ms. Winters said. She narrowed her eyes. "Was it an upsetting dream, like a nightmare?"

"No. I enjoyed it mostly. It's just that it felt really real—realer than any dream I've ever had."

"Well, some people do dream more vividly during different parts of their lives," Ms. Winters said. "I know I had some crazy, real-seeming dreams when I was pregnant. Blame it on the hormones." She smiled.

Maisie smiled back at her, though, she felt that bordered on Too Much Information. "I guess I'm curious what my dream meant."

"Ah," Ms. Winters said. "Well, there are different schools of thought on what dreams mean. Freud thought they were a kind of wish fulfillment combined with some of the stuff that was floating through your brain from the day before. Jung believed that dreams were a natural expression of our imaginations. But of course, both of those guys were writing a long time ago, and lots of people have had other ideas since then. If you like, I could bring you some books from home tomorrow."

"That would be great," Maisie said. "Thanks."

Wish fulfillment. For the rest of the school day, Maisie thought about that phrase. Maybe that's what her dream had been. She wished to live in another time, and her dream had made that wish come true . . . at least until her alarm went off.

Maisie wanted to go back to her dream. She wanted to walk the cobblestone streets again, to visit with Violet, to maybe see what the tea dance was like. She put on her pajamas and brushed her teeth and wished she had asked Ms. Winters if there was some way to guide your brain to return to a dream it had had before.

Maisie tried to remember what she had done last night before having the dream. She hadn't eaten or drunk anything right before sleeping. She actually hadn't even fallen asleep on purpose; she had just dozed off. Maisie took out her little-used phone and texted Abby.

Maisie: Hey.

Abby: Hey. You never text. Are u ok?

Maisie: Yeah, I was just wondering if you've ever dreamed about the same thing twice.

Abby: Are you sure you're ok?

Maisie: Yeah. I just had this dream last night set in the Victorian era. It was interesting, and I want to go back and pick up where I left off.

Abby: Isn't that when that brooch you got is from? The Victorian era?

Maisie: Abby, you're a genius!

Of course. Last night when she had the dream, she had fallen asleep wearing the chatelaine, which came from the same era in which her dream took place. She laughed at herself for thinking something so superstitious, but then on impulse, she went to her jewelry box, took out the chatelaine, and pinned it to her pajama top. She couldn't believe she was doing something so silly, but what could it hurt? She climbed into bed and snuggled down under the covers.

"Well, look at how lovely you are!" the middle-aged woman said. She was wearing a long, plain, dark gray dress, and her salt-and-pepper hair was pulled back in a severe bun. "As fresh and dewy as a spring rose!"

"Thank you," Maisie said. She turned to look at herself in the full-length mirror that was beside her in the bedroom she presumed was hers. It was a very fancy, very feminine room. The wallpaper was splashed

148

with red roses, and there was a large canopy bed with deep red curtains that could be drawn for privacy.

The flowing, floor-length gown Maisie was wearing was rose pink. The round neckline was trimmed with beautiful but scratchy cream-colored lace, and the sleeves were hugely puffy, with more lace on the cuffs. Her hair was piled on top of her head except for two wavy tendrils, which hung down at her temples. A cameo pendant just like one she had seen at the flea market jewelry booth hung at the hollow of her throat. The chatelaine was pinned to the bodice of her dress. It always seemed to just appear on everything she wore.

"Are you sure you want to wear that brooch?" the woman said. "You don't want the pin to damage such fine fabric."

"I do want to wear it," Maisie said. The truth was, she was pretty sure that if she took it off, it would just come back again, and that thought disturbed her so much that she didn't want to risk it.

"Well, your mother's necklace adds a very special touch," the woman said. "She would be so proud of you. Shall we show your father how pretty you look before we go?"

Maisie smiled and nodded. She was fairly certain they were going to the tea dance. And she guessed that this woman was her governess. Maisie wished she knew the woman's name.

Maisie followed the governess out of the bedroom and into the hall. The walls were papered green with a gold brocade pattern. Mirrors and family portraits hung on the walls. It looked to be a large house. There were four doors in the hallway, each of which, Maisie figured, probably led to a lavish bedroom. She tried her best to follow along and look like she knew where she was going.

Her governess stopped her when they reached the top of an elegant, curving wooden staircase. "Wait right there," she said. "I want your father to watch you come down the stairs."

Maisie thought it was a weird idea, but she nodded. Nodding, she was finding, came in handy in this dreamscape. It was better to nod quietly than to accidentally say the wrong thing. And people liked it when you appeared to agree with them.

She stood at the top of the stairs and saw her governess approaching with a bearded middle-aged man dressed in a dark suit with a shiny pearl-gray vest. He was smoking a pipe.

"Here he is, Maisie!" the governess called. "Let him have a look at you."

"You always like to put on a show, don't you, Harper?" the man said, chuckling. "It's like every day is a day at the circus."

Harper, Maisie noted to herself. *The governess's*

name is Harper. There was a lot to learn in this new—
yet old—environment.

Maisie walked down the stairs slowly with a slight
smile on her face, like she had seen an actress do in an old
movie once. She walked slowly, partly because she wanted
to look elegant, but mostly because she was afraid of tripping on her long gown and falling down the stairs.

"Beautiful," her father said, shaking his head like he
couldn't believe what he was seeing. "Such a beautiful,
elegant young lady. I wish your mother could see you."

"I said the same thing," the governess said.

"Thank you, Papa," Maisie said, then kissed his
cheek. It felt a bit odd to kiss him since she had just met
him, but it seemed like the right gesture.

"I called a cab for you ladies," Papa said, smiling.
"I didn't want a long walk to spoil your fresh clothes. I
gave him instructions to pick you up promptly at seven
when the dance is over."

"That was very generous of you, Mr. Lawrence,"
Harper said.

"Well, it's a special occasion, isn't it?" Papa said.
"Have fun, ladies, but be on your best behavior."

Harper giggled a little. Maisie couldn't imagine
this prim woman ever being on anything but her best
behavior.

The cab waiting outside was a horse-drawn carriage for two, which was, Maisie supposed, what would

have been called a cab in this time and place. What had she been expecting? A yellow taxi?

She very much wanted to pet the horse but didn't know if that would be considered strange. People here probably thought of horses as forms of transportation rather than as beautiful, lovable animals. The driver stepped down from his perch and offered his hand to help Maisie into the carriage. He didn't offer his hand to Harper, perhaps because she was a servant, which struck Maisie as unfair. It was probably harder for the middle-aged governess to climb into a carriage than it was for Maisie.

The ride was bumpy, but the view of the Victorian homes and shops was spectacular. Maisie spotted businesses you'd never see in a modern town, a blacksmith's shop, a milliner (which she was pretty sure meant a hat maker), and a store selling *dry goods*, whatever those were.

"I'm sure you would be happier if I weren't coming with you, but your papa wouldn't have it any other way," Harper said.

Maisie actually couldn't imagine what she would do if Harper wasn't with her. It was only by following her lead that Maisie managed to look like she knew what she was doing. "On the contrary," Maisie said, trying to make her speech more formal to better fit in. "I am very happy to have you with me, Harper."

To Maisie's surprise, the governess looked as if

Maisie had slapped her. *"Harper?"* she said, sounding hurt and offended. "Have you gotten to be such a great, big girl that you won't call me *Guvvy* anymore?"

"Oh!" said Maisie, desperate to cover her misstep. "Of course not . . . Guvvy."

"Good," Guvvy said, sniffling slightly. "I always want you to call me *Guvvy*. Even when you're married and I'm taking care of your little ones."

Maisie reached over and patted the older woman's hand. "I promise I will. Even if I'm eighty years old."

Guvvy laughed. "If you live to be eighty, then I'll be a hundred and five. I don't expect you'll be calling me much then, except old bones!"

After an hour-long ride out of the city and into the country, the cab pulled up in front of a sprawling stone mansion. There were towers and turrets and architectural details Maisie didn't know the names of. Whatever they were, they sure were fancy. Maisie's home in this dream was lavish, but this place was palatial.

The cab driver stopped in front of the home's double doors and helped Maisie out of the cab.

"I'll be back for you at seven, Miss," he said.

Maisie thanked him. Nodding at people and thanking them—those were the two things that were getting her by. She was going to get the reputation of being a very agreeable person.

"You make your entrance, dear," Guvvy said. "I'll just follow along behind and blend into the woodwork."

"No, walk in with me," Maisie said, taking Guvvy's hand.

Guvvy looked confused, but maybe a little pleased, too.

A butler in a coat with tails showed them in. Maisie felt like she was in a movie.

The room where the dance was being held was so large she couldn't believe it was in a person's house. Along the back wall of the room was a long table spread with a spectacular assortment of tiny sandwiches, roasted meats, fruit tarts, butter cookies, meringues, and a big pink cake decorated with roses. There was lemonade, fruit punch, tea, and coffee, but also bottles of champagne resting in buckets of ice. Maisie had never seen anything so elegant. She felt sorry for the girls in her regular life who thought that the high school prom was the height of glamour. A smelly old high school gym decorated with crepe paper and balloons couldn't compare to grandeur like this.

It was a lovely room, lit only by the sunlight streaming through the windows, the floor polished to a high sheen. But the loveliest sight to Maisie was the girls in their beautiful dresses. In spring shades of lilac and daffodil yellow and morning glory blue, they were like a flower garden come to life. While Maisie was taking it all in, a girl in a purple dress ran up to her.

"Maisie!" she said. Her blonde hair was in an elaborate updo with violets threaded through the curls.

"Violet!" Maisie said back.

Violet took both of Maisie's hands. "I can't believe how beautiful you look."

"You look beautiful, too," Maisie said. "I love the flowers in your hair."

Violet touched her head and blushed. "Thank you." A swell of music came from the small orchestra on the far end of the room. "Oh! The dancing's about to start!"

Guvvy patted Maisie's shoulder. "You have a nice time, dear. I'm going to help myself to refreshments, then go sit with the other governesses."

Maisie watched as the pastel-clad young ladies paired off with young gentlemen in suits with frock coats that almost reached their knees, then the couple sailed gracefully around the dance floor. Maisie didn't know whether or not to wish someone would ask her to dance. She didn't know any of the steps, and she did well enough to manage to walk in a long dress and petticoats, let alone dance. But she didn't want to be a wallflower, either.

After a few songs, a thin, pleasant-looking young man approached her. "Would you care to dance?" he asked.

Maisie gave him an embarrassed smile. "I'm afraid I'm not very good at it."

He smiled back. There was a gap between his two front teeth, which made him look friendlier somehow. "Nor am I. We'll make a perfect pair. How many people's toes can we step on, do you think?"

Maisie laughed and walked with him onto the dance floor. Once the orchestra started playing, Maisie felt the strangest sensation. Somehow, her feet knew exactly what to do. They knew what kind of dance it was and what the steps were. Maisie didn't understand how her feet suddenly knew more than her brain did, but she was perfectly happy to follow their lead. It was like she was a puppet and someone else was pulling the strings.

"You sell yourself short, Maisie," the young man said. "You are an excellent dancer."

Maisie had actually been about to introduce herself to the young man, but apparently he already knew her. She, however, had no idea what his name might be, and there was no polite way to ask him. "Thank you," she said. "I'm kind of surprised by how well I'm dancing, actually. Perhaps it's because I have such a good partner."

He smiled. "No, that couldn't be it. Perhaps it's just that I'm so bad I make you look even better."

Maisie laughed. This guy, whatever his name might be, was certainly likeable.

Once the song was over, he asked, "Could I interest you in a cup of punch?"

"That would be lovely," Maisie said, trying to speak the proper lingo.

They made their way to the refreshment table, and he dipped them each a cup of punch from the cut-glass punch bowl. She took a sip. It was tepid but delicious. It tasted of fresh strawberries, like a sweeter version of the smoothies her mom made for her in real life.

"There you are!" a male voice said.

Maisie looked up to see Edwin standing in front of her. He was wearing an emerald-green cravat, and his mustache had been waxed to the point of stiffness.

"Hello, Edwin," Maisie said, trying not to sound as annoyed as she felt. She had actually been enjoying the company of Mr. Whatever His Name Was.

"May I have the next dance?" Edwin asked.

Maisie wanted desperately to say no, but Violet was her friend. She couldn't offend Violet by being rude to her brother. Manners were everything in this society. "I would be delighted," she lied.

"Do save another dance for me later in the evening," her former dance partner said.

"I will," Maisie said as Edwin took her hand and dragged her to the dance floor.

This was a faster, more energetic song than the

one she had danced to before, but once again, her feet knew exactly what to do. Edwin held her hand and her waist too tightly, as if he were afraid she might get away.

"You look beautiful tonight, Maisie," Edwin said. "I can feel the other gents' eyes on me because they wish they were dancing with you."

"I'm sure that's not true, but it's very flattering," Maisie said. Something about Edwin's compliments felt forced, as if he had rehearsed saying them at home in front of the mirror while he was waxing his mustache.

They sailed past Violet on the dance floor who called at them, "It makes me so happy to see the two of you together!"

Maisie smiled at her friend. Why was Violet happy to see her dancing with Edwin? Maybe he had a hard time finding dance partners at events like this. Maybe the other girls found him as unpleasant as Maisie did.

Maisie danced with several other young men, then had another dance with the nice young man whose name she didn't know. The two of them visited the buffet, where Maisie filled her plate with what she was sure was an unladylike amount of food.

"These little sandwiches are always interesting," her nameless companion said, "because you have no idea what you're getting until you bite into one."

Maisie smiled. "How suspenseful." She nibbled the

corner of a sandwich. "Hmm . . . ham and, I think, pickle?" she said.

Nameless popped a whole sandwich into his mouth and chewed thoughtfully.

"What kind is it?" Maisie asked.

Nameless swallowed, then said, "I have no earthly idea. It was delicious, though!"

Maisie laughed. She forked up a bite from the large piece of pink cake she had put on her plate. It tasted strangely floral and perfumy.

"You're making quite a face there," Nameless said, smiling.

"Oh, am I? I'm sorry. The cake just wasn't what I was expecting. Since it was pink, I thought it would be strawberry."

"Oh, no, that's a rose cake," Nameless said. "That's why I didn't take a piece. They're very popular, but why is beyond me. It's not as if people go around chewing on rosebushes."

Maisie felt a hand on her shoulder.

"I believe you've monopolized this young lady for long enough, Thomas."

She turned around to find the source of the voice, though, she already knew who it was.

"I beg your pardon, Edwin," Thomas-Formerly-Known-as-Nameless said. "Her company was so charming I forgot to keep track of time."

"Well, I'm here because you needed a reminder," Edwin said, his voice as cold as an icicle. He reached over to the buffet table and touched the handle of the large knife that lay next to the roast beef. "Sometimes reminders can be painful."

Thomas looked Edwin in the eye. "There's no need for such theatrics, Edwin. I am more than willing to excuse myself so you can ask the young lady if she cares to dance."

Maisie didn't want Thomas to go, and she definitely didn't want to dance with Edwin. But if dancing with him was the only way to prevent Edwin from carving up Thomas like roast beef, then dance she would.

In the cab on the way home, Guvvy rattled off all the gossip she had accumulated from watching the festivities with the other governesses. She seemed a little giddy, and Maisie wondered if she had helped herself to a glass or two of champagne.

"Edwin Breedlove seemed to be enjoying your company this evening," Guvvy said.

"Oh." Edwin was the last person Maisie wanted to talk about. "I think it's just that he feels comfortable with me because I'm friends with his sister."

"Oh," Guvvy said with a mysterious smile. "Is that what you think it is?"

With Guvvy's help, Maisie changed out of her party dress and into a loose white nightgown. Being out of the corset was a huge relief, though the stays had marked the skin along her ribs and waist with long pink welts. Maisie climbed into the large wooden bed with its canopy and curtains. The bed itself was surprisingly soft. *This has certainly been a long dream,* Maisie thought. *I guess when I wake up, it'll be for real, and I'll be in my real bed in my real room.*

CHAPTER 5

When Maisie woke up, the first things she saw were the canopy over her head and the curtains around her. Okay, so she hadn't really woken up, which was weird. She had never had a dream with such a long time frame. It had started out feeling like a movie, and now it felt like a miniseries.

There was a soft knock on the door.

"Come in," Maisie said.

A startlingly young maid whom Maisie had never seen before came in carrying a tray. "Mrs. Harper said you should have your breakfast here while I get your bath ready. After you bathe and dress, she'll come up and get you for a meeting with your father."

The word *meeting* seemed strangely formal for any type of conversation one would have with a parent. But then again, a lot of things in this dream world were strangely formal. Even breakfast was more elaborate than she was used to, served to her on a fussy little tray by an aproned maid who couldn't be a day over fourteen. There was a boiled egg in some kind of weird egg holder, a metal rack holding slices of buttered toast, a little glass dish of jam, and a dainty cup of coffee with a miniature pitcher of cream.

She nibbled the toast and sipped the coffee. People drank endless cups of coffee and tea in this world! She would kill for a mocha from Java Jive right now, or even for some very cold water from the metal tumbler she carried with her to school. Things that were supposed to be cold here were always tepid. She was gaining an appreciation for the wonders of modern refrigeration.

In a few minutes, the maid returned. "Your bath is ready, Miss."

"Thank you," Maisie said. Once again, she was in that awkward position where she should have known the name of the person she was talking to but didn't.

The bathtub was deep and massive, with ornamental clawed feet that looked like they could belong to a gryphon or a dragon.

"Shall I stay to help you, Miss?" the maid asked.

"Wait—what? No," Maisie said, more forcefully than she should have. "I mean, no, thank you."

What was the maid going to help her do? Wash

herself? Shouldn't people know how to do that by the time they were far younger than Maisie's age?

After the maid was gone, Maisie got into the tub and was soon soaking up to her neck. She had never been in a tub so large before. That was the thing about the Victorian era—everything was bigger and fancier than it needed to be. She looked around the bathroom, at the toilet with a golden pull chain, the glazed tile walls, the huge mirror over the sink, and the most confusing item—a plush chaise longue that seemed like it would make more sense in some other room. There was no doubt about it: Here more was definitely more.

There was a hard rapping on the bathroom door. "Maisie!" It was Guvvy's voice. "You need to finish up in the tub and get dressed. We have to be downstairs in your father's study in fifteen minutes."

Maisie splashed some hot water on her face and got out of the tub. The towel was rougher and scratchier than she was used to. She patted herself dry and put her nightgown back on. When she went to her room, Guvvy had laid out her elaborate underwear and a forest-green dress with a small floral print. It was what Guvvy described as an "everyday dress," but with its lacey trim and fitted bodice, it still looked quite fancy to Maisie. "Oh, we should have started getting ready much earlier!" Guvvy said. "And you've let your hair get all wet. How can we possibly make it look presentable?"

"Why does it matter how I look? I'm just going downstairs," Maisie said. On days when she stayed home in real life, sometimes she never changed out of her pajamas.

"It matters more than you know," Guvvy said. "A lady must always look her best. You never know when you might be visited by someone on whom you want to make a good impression!"

Maisie let Guvvy help her into her torturous underwear. It was a strange thing. Everyone was so modest—they wouldn't say tables or chairs had legs because they were afraid it might sound too naughty, and yet they let their servants undress, wash, and dress them all the time.

Guvvy took a hairbrush and went to work on Maisie's hair, frowning as she attacked the damp tangles. Finally, she settled on braiding it and pinning it up in a braided bun. "I suppose that will have to do," she said with a sigh.

Again Maisie thought, *I'm just going downstairs.*

Maisie followed Guvvy out of her room, down the stairs, and through the hallway past the foyer. She heard the sound of men laughing from behind a closed door.

Guvvy gave the door a gentle knock.

"Come in, ladies!" Papa's voice called. Maisie wondered whom the other voice she had heard belonged to.

Papa was sitting at a big oak desk stacked with books and papers. A man whose back was to Maisie was sitting in the armchair across from the desk. "Just in time!" Papa said, smiling widely. "We were just discussing the terms of your engagement."

Maisie thought she either didn't hear him correctly, or maybe he was using the word in a way she wasn't familiar with. "My what?"

"Your engagement, you silly girl!" Papa said. "To this fine gentleman right here."

The man in the chair turned around to smile at Maisie. She took in the blond hair, the sideburns, the mustache.

"Edwin?" she said. She felt the toast and tea from breakfast lurch in her stomach. There had to be some kind of mistake.

"You're such a little trickster," Papa said, smiling, "acting like you're unaware of this arrangement when you've known about it for months."

Guvvy placed a hand on Maisie's forehead. "You're not feeling ill, are you, my dear?"

Maisie pushed her hand away. "You don't understand. I can't be engaged. I'm only fifteen!"

"Well, naturally, the wedding won't take place until after your sixteenth birthday," Papa said, as if sixteen were a perfectly reasonable age to get married.

Maisie turned to Guvvy—Guvvy, who acted like a

mother in a lot of ways and clearly cared about her a great deal. "Surely you don't approve of this?" she said.

Guvvy smiled. "It's not my place to approve or disapprove. But I will say any girl should be pleased to make a match with a young man as promising as Mr. Edwin Breedlove!"

It was a nightmare. That's what it was—a literal nightmare. Maisie just had to make herself wake up. Usually she could talk herself awake when she was having a bad dream. *This is just a dream. It's time to wake up. This is just a dream. It's time to wake up.* She repeated it to herself over and over again, and nothing happened except that everyone in the room was looking at her with expressions that were both confused and concerned.

Sometimes when she was dreaming, she could will herself to move and that would wake her up. Once she had done this and woken up on the floor. This led to a bruise on her thigh, but it was worth it. She twisted her waist back and forth, flailing her arms and screaming, "Wake up, wake up, wake up!"

Papa's expression had shifted from mild concern to genuine worry. "Maybe you should fetch her the medicine, Harper," he said.

Within what felt like a minute, a spoonful of something strong tasting was being forced between her lips. Soon, everything went black.

The next thing Maisie knew, she was lying on the

couch in the living room with Papa, Guvvy, and Edwin standing over her.

"It's no cause for alarm, Edwin," Papa said. "Young ladies are often overcome by emotion."

"You seem to forget I have a sister," Edwin said, and everyone laughed.

"Here, see if you can sit up and drink some water," Guvvy said, holding out a glass.

Maisie allowed Guvvy to help her up and took a few small sips.

"Better?" Guvvy asked.

Maisie nodded. But she was not better. Her head felt fuzzy and light, as if someone had replaced her brain with cotton candy.

"May I have just a moment with my betrothed?" Edwin asked Papa.

"Of course," Papa said. "I'll be in my study."

Maisie was grateful that Guvvy showed no signs of going anywhere.

"A moment *alone*, if you please, Mrs. Harper," Edwin said.

"Of course, sir," Guvvy said. "I'll be in the kitchen if you need me, Maisie."

Maisie wanted to go with Guvvy to the kitchen, but she was starting to understand that however good Guvvy's intentions were, she didn't really have the power to protect her in this situation.

Edwin sat down beside her. He grabbed her wrist, hard. His face was red with rage, and his words came out in a whispered hiss. "Now, see here, girly, you made a fool of me in front of your father. I will not tolerate that kind of behavior again."

Maisie jerked her hand away. "Is this the way you talk to someone you love?"

Edwin laughed bitterly. "*Love?* You think that is what this is about . . . love? I may make tender declarations to you in front of your papa and Guvvy and the foolish girls at the tea dance, but believe me, this arrangement is strictly a financial one."

She tried to concentrate, to make her thoughts less fuzzy. "Well, then, I'll tell Papa and Guvvy what you just said!"

"Oh, you can try if you like, but they'll never believe you. I have them both eating out of my hand, and besides, the sooner your papa gets you married off, the happier he'll be. With your mama in the ground, he can start a new life for himself. No widower wants to be encumbered with a spinster for a daughter."

"This is insane!" Maisie said. "I'm a person. I have choices!"

Edwin leaned closer to her face. Anyone who didn't know better would think he was being romantic. "The only choice you have in this situation, my dearest betrothed, is to keep your mouth shut and cooperate. If you do, chances are good that no harm will come to you. But if you open that little mouth of yours to your papa, to your Guvvy, or to anyone else, well, I'm afraid I cannot be held responsible for what might happen to you. Terrible accidents can happen to young girls when they're unprotected." He stood up and gave a mock-gentlemanly bow. "Good day to you, my dearest. I will see myself out."

Maisie put her head in her hands. It felt heavy with the weight of all that she was starting to understand. She knew now that none of this was a dream. Somehow, she was really here and this was really happening, and if there was a way out, she couldn't see it.

CHAPTER 6

"Feeling better today?" Guvvy asked as she stood at Maisie's bedside.

"Yes, thank you," Maisie said.

The truth was, Maisie hadn't slept all night. She had alternated between lying in bed and pacing, desperately trying to think of a way to escape. A way to escape a marriage she didn't consent to and a time she was trapped in. Was there even a way she could get out of the 1800s and go back to the life she had always known? Even if there wasn't, even if she had to stay here and live out her life as a Victorian girl, never seeing her real family again, she had to figure out a way to avoid being Mrs. Edwin Breedlove.

She wasn't sure how, but she kept thinking the secret was in the chatelaine. If the chatelaine had brought her here, could the chatelaine take her back?

"You'll have breakfast in the dining room with your papa this morning," Guvvy said. "He wants to see you looking well, so wash your face and let's get you dressed."

"Yes, Guvvy." Maisie got out of bed and went over to the basin of warm water the maid left in her bedroom every morning. She dipped a scratchy washcloth in the water and wiped her face and then under her arms. Apparently there was no deodorant in this era, and the clothes were not made of breathable fabric. Maisie was tired of smelling her own sweat.

Guvvy helped her put on a corset, lacing it so tightly that Maisie gasped for breath. The chocolate-brown dress that Guvvy had selected for her had about a million buttons that had to be fastened with a buttonhook. *No wonder it was so hard for women in this era to make any contributions to society*, Maisie thought. *It took them too long to get dressed.*

"There," Guvvy said when the last button was finally done. "Now, sit down at the vanity, and we'll see what we can do with your hair."

Maisie cooperated fully. One thing she had decided during her sleepless night was that arguing and appearing to be uncooperative in this situation worked against her. When she had protested her engagement yesterday, she had ended up drugged—what was that stuff

Guvvy gave her, anyway?—and unconscious on the couch. If she openly resisted them, they would just physically overpower her. The trick (and it was no easy trick) was to appear to be an obedient, unquestioning girl, all the while secretly plotting her escape.

And so Maisie sat and waited patiently while Guvvy ran the rough brush through her hair, then divided it into sections, which she twisted up on top of Maisie's head and decorated with a hair ribbon. The silly style reminded Maisie of a little yappy dog that had just gone to the groomer, but she smiled and said, "That looks nice."

Guvvy smiled. "I did do a rather good job, didn't I?"

At breakfast, Maisie smiled and said, "Good morning, Papa," then said yes to everything the maid offered to put on her plate: the eggs, the porridge, the toast, the ham, and the bacon. *Who had ham and bacon at the same meal?* Maisie wondered. *Did these people have something against pigs?* Maisie forced down the heavy food and thought longingly of the light fruit smoothies her mother made her for breakfast back at home. Everything there seemed so relaxed and calm. Would she ever have breakfast with her real mom and dad again? Would she ever see them again at all, for that matter? Maisie fought back tears.

Papa looked out from behind his newspaper and said, "Annie is going downtown to do the marketing this morning. Let her know if there's anything you need."

Annie must be the maid's name, Maisie thought. She racked her brain. Was there anything Annie could get that would possibly help her situation?

An idea popped into Maisie's head. Violet. Maybe Violet would help her. Yes, Violet was Edwin's sister, but she was also clearly Maisie's best friend in this world. If Maisie could be tactful about her situation, not saying she was afraid of Edwin, but only that she wasn't ready for marriage, then maybe Violet could use her influence as Edwin's sister to get Maisie out of this situation.

When Annie came back to the table, offering fish, of all things, Maisie said, "Annie, if I were to write a note to my friend Violet, could you deliver it to her when you go to town?"

"Of course, Miss," Annie said.

"Thank you, Annie," Maisie said. "I'll write it as soon as I finish breakfast."

"I'll stop by your room to collect it," Annie said.

Maisie sat down at the writing desk in her room, where she found stationery and envelopes. There was a metal pen, but when she tried to write with it, it didn't have any ink. Then she saw the inkwell sitting in a special indentation in the desk and understood. But she had never used an inkwell before and wasn't sure how far to dip the pen into it and how to avoid dripping ink everywhere and making a big mess. She touched the very tip of the pen against the surface of the ink. She was nervous about how to use the pen—she didn't know how hard to press down or how to make the writing flow. But as soon as she touched pen to paper, she knew exactly what to do. It was just like when her feet had known what to do on the dance floor. She only needed to think the words, and they showed up on the paper. Her hand felt out of her control, but it guided the pen gracefully. She tried to muster all the good manners and floweriness she could manage and wrote:

My dear Violet,

Could you meet me on the bench near the entrance of the city park today at three o'clock? I wish to speak privately.

Your devoted friend,
Maisie

She folded the note, placed it in an envelope, and wrote Violet's name on it. When Annie gently knocked on her door, Maisie gave her the note.

Maisie waited on the park bench. She had told Guvvy she was going out for thirty minutes of fresh air. She hoped that Violet would show up and would be sympathetic. If anybody needed a friend right now, Maisie did. She thought of Abby back home. Abby might not be the coolest or most stylish-looking friend, but Maisie could always count on Abby to be on her side. She hoped Violet was the same.

In a few minutes, Violet came flouncing down the sidewalk, wearing a butter-yellow gown with a matching hat and parasol. "Oh my goodness," Violet said. "Look at you, out in the sun with no parasol! Why, you'll freckle most terribly!"

Maisie remembered reading in her *Fashion Through the Decades* book that Victorian women were notorious for avoiding the sun because being pale was the height of fashion. Some women had even drunk small quantities of arsenic to achieve a stylish deathly pallor. "Oh, I'll be fine," Maisie said.

"Nonsense, you can share mine!" Violet said, squeezing close to Maisie on the bench so they were both somewhat shaded by the tiny umbrella. "I was so excited when your maid brought your note," Violet said. "A secret meeting—I'm so curious what it's about!"

"Thank you for meeting me," Maisie said. "Sometimes you just need to talk to a girlfriend, you know?"

"I do," Violet said. "Especially when you want to talk about . . . a wedding!" Violet collapsed into a fit of giggles.

This wasn't the response Maisie had been hoping for. "Well, that's sort of what it's about. My father met with your brother yesterday about his plans to marry me."

"I know he did." Violet smiled and grabbed Maisie's hand. "Can you imagine it, Maisie? Once you're married to Edwin, we won't just be best friends. We'll be *sisters*."

This definitely wasn't going well. Maisie took a deep breath. "See, here's the thing, Violet. I love the idea of you and I being sisters. But I'm not so crazy about the idea of marrying your brother. Or marrying anyone right now. I'm too young." To tell the truth, Maisie hadn't ever been on a real date. Jumping into marriage was definitely skipping a lot of steps.

Violet smiled. "Better to marry too young than too old! My cousin Grace is twenty-six and unwed. She's well on her way to being an old maid!"

Maisie had hoped she could handle the situation without making it about Edwin personally, but Violet didn't seem to be hearing her more-polite attempts at extricating herself from the situation. "Violet, I don't want to endanger our friendship, and I know this puts you in an awkward situation, but I don't want to marry your brother."

Violet's eyes widened in apparent surprise. "But why wouldn't you want to marry Edwin? He's a very promising gentleman, and he absolutely adores you."

Maisie felt tears spring to her eyes. Violet was a good, trusting soul. Of course she thought the best of her brother. "No, he doesn't, Violet. He doesn't adore me. I hate to tell you this because I don't want to hurt your relationship with him, but he told me that his marriage to me would be for strictly financial reasons."

With great force, Violet threw her parasol. It hit a nearby tree and smashed into splinters.

Violet was up on her feet. "He said that, did he?" Her voice was different somehow, more adult, without a trace of her usual giggly girlishness. "That's the trouble with my brother. He always lets the mask slip."

Maisie was thoroughly confused by this person standing before her who looked like Violet but seemed to have an entirely different personality. "I'm sorry. I'm afraid I don't understand," Maisie said.

"Well, that's actually not the problem," Violet said. "You weren't supposed to understand, but now you do. Edwin isn't as good as I am at playing the long game. Someone will make him lose his temper, and he'll forget to play the part and reveal everything. I suppose that's what he did with you."

"So this is like . . . a con? And you're part of it?" Maisie said. She was starting to feel like she was locked in an already small room and the walls were closing in.

Violet shook her head. "Of course I'm part of it, you stupid girl. I'm the one who lures the rich girl in by becoming her best friend, then I just happen to introduce her to my charming brother—"

"You talk like this is something you've done before," Maisie said. The idea scared her. She wondered how fast she could run in this ridiculous getup if she needed to.

"Don't put words in my mouth, girly. I said nothing of the kind," Violet said. "Now that you know it's a game, all you have to do is play by the rules. Be a good girl and marry my brother so he can get the very generous dowry your father has promised him, and don't say a word to anyone about the marriage being a sham. If you're nice to us, we'll be nice to you." Violet took Maisie's trembling hand in hers. "You keep quiet, I'll keep Edwin on his best behavior, and I'll be as soft and sweet as a kitten. But breathe one word to anyone, especially the police, and you'll find that this kitten has claws." Violet raked her fingernails hard down the back of Maisie's hand, producing four bloody scratch marks.

Maisie snatched her hand away. Tears had sprung to her eyes. "I thought you were my friend!"

Violet's smile was different than the one Maisie had known before. "That's part of the game, girly. But you play along and give us what we want, and you and I can still be friends. Trust me. You don't want me as your enemy."

CHAPTER 7

Maisie paced the length of her dark bedroom in her nightgown, thinking. She now had not only Edwin to fear, but Violet. Violet whom she had liked and trusted. Or at least, she had liked and trusted the version of Violet that had been presented to her, which apparently had very little to do with the real Violet.

Everything was overwhelming and confusing, but one thing was clear: She was all alone, and nobody was going to help her. If she was going to get out of this dangerous situation, she would have to figure it out by herself.

The chatelaine. The thought popped into her head like a bursting soap bubble. *It was falling asleep wearing the chatelaine that got me here.*

During the day, the chatelaine showed up on

whatever uncomfortable dress Guvvy stuffed her into, but it was never on her nightgown. The chatelaine was in a small jewelry box on her dresser. It was too dark to see—Maisie was coming to appreciate what a fantastic invention modern electric lighting was—but she groped around until she felt the box and was able to open it. She took out the chatelaine, pinned it on, and made her way back to bed.

Now came the hard part: relaxing enough so that she could go to sleep.

After a fitful night, Maisie opened her eyes and saw, once again, the canopy and the curtains. She wept tears of frustration and despair.

"My goodness, are you crying?" Guvvy said when she came in to help Maisie dress.

Maisie didn't feel like she needed to say yes since the answer was visibly obvious.

"You know what I was thinking?" Guvvy said, smoothing Maisie's hair in a motherly way. "Since your birthday is in June, what if we had your wedding on your birthday? It could be a double celebration, with a wedding cake and a birthday cake!"

Maisie cried harder. Her birthday was only a month away.

"I understand that you're nervous about getting married," Guvvy said. "But a girl has to be practical about her future. I was just a year older than you when I married Mr. Harper, you know."

"And you're happy?" Maisie asked.

"He's a good man," Guvvy said. "He's never struck me. He holds down a job and pays his debts. He doesn't drink." She was quiet for a second, then repeated, "He's a good man."

Maisie noticed that Guvvy didn't say she was happy.

After breakfast, Maisie asked if she could go outside for some fresh air. Guvvy allowed it, but insisted she carry a parasol to keep the sun off her skin. And so now she was walking down the street carrying a frilly tiny umbrella, which made her feel absolutely ridiculous.

She had wanted to go out so she could think. She went to the park bench where she had sat with Violet and ran back through their conversation in her head. When Violet had spoken of her role in luring the rich girl to be her friend and then introducing her to her brother, it had sounded like something she and her brother had done before. If this was the case, was there any way to prove that they were running a scam? If she could prove it, then surely Papa would call off the wedding, which, while it wouldn't return her to her normal life, would at least rid her of her most-pressing problem.

Maisie jumped up from the park bench. She abandoned her parasol—maybe some birds could use it to build an extra-fancy nest—and hurried to Main Street.

She wasn't sure how people did research here. There was no Internet, that's for sure. But walking around town she had noticed the offices of *The Star Tribune*, the local weekly newspaper. Stopping by seemed worth a shot.

The Star Tribune office smelled pleasantly of ink and cheap paper. A husky man in a rumpled suit sat behind a cluttered desk near the entrance. "Good morning, Miss. How can I help you?" he asked.

"I was wondering," Maisie began, "is there any way to look at old issues of the newspaper?"

"Oh, you'll need the morgue, then," he said, smiling like he had just made a pleasant suggestion.

"The morgue?" This was certainly taking a dark turn. If she crossed Edwin and Violet, that's where she feared she'd end up, anyway.

The man chuckled. "I didn't mean to alarm you. It's newspaper slang. The morgue is the room where we keep old issues of the paper. Here, let me show you."

The man led Maisie down the hall and into a dusty room filled with wooden filing cabinets. "The papers are organized by year. Was there any particular issue you were looking for?"

"No, sir," Maisie said, feeling foolish because she didn't really know what she was looking for. "I'm just working on a project . . . for my tutor." In the past, she had always found that when you told adults you were doing something for a school project, they would let you get away with anything.

"Well, you just make yourself at home here, and let me know if you have any questions. The papers are filed chronologically. Please make sure you keep them in order."

"Yes, sir. Thank you."

For the most part, *The Star Tribune* was not hard-hitting journalism. There were stories about garden parties and dogs that ran away but were found by their owners and a column by the minister of the Presbyterian church. Maisie had thought everyone's speech was ridiculously ornate and flowery, but the written English in the paper was even more so. She pored through issue after issue, hoping to find something pertinent, growing more and more frustrated that there was no way to look for information except for exhaustive digging. If she ever got to return to her life, she would never take search engines for granted again.

After nearly four hours of perusing back issues, Maisie spotted a headline from an issue that had been published three years prior: LOCAL MAN CLEARED OF ALL CHARGES, WIFE'S DROWNING RULED AN ACCIDENT.

She read on:

A cloud of suspicion has hung over Edwin Breedlove since his new bride's drowning in a boating accident last week. The deceased, Mrs. Elizabeth Breedlove (née Simpson) allegedly fell overboard and drowned when a romantic afternoon on a rowboat with her husband took a tragic turn. Mrs. Breedlove's parents, however, suspected foul play, saying that as soon as Mr. Breedlove received a sizable dowry, his behavior toward his new wife was often erratic and cruel. However, the medical examiner has ruled Mrs. Breedlove's death an accident, saying that the blows she received to the head, which her parents had cited as a sign of possible foul play, were consistent with injuries she could have received accidentally hitting her head on the boat as she fell from it.

Mr. Breedlove was not available for comment; however, his sister, Miss Violet Breedlove, stated, "I am very thankful that my brother's good name has been restored. Now all that we ask is that he be allowed his privacy so that he may mourn the tragic passing of his dear wife."

Maisie knew the trauma to Elizabeth Breedlove's head was not caused by accidentally bumping it as she fell off the boat. The picture in her mind was so clear she knew it was right: Elizabeth, after Edwin shoved her off the boat, her heavy dress becoming heavier with water, tried to climb back aboard, and Edwin hit her on the head with the oar again and again and again.

Maisie felt sick. She took deep breaths, trying to stop the urge to throw up. It was very hard to take satisfactory deep breaths while wearing a corset.

She wished she could take a picture of the article, but since she couldn't, she folded the newspaper and stuffed it in the waistband of her petticoat. She felt guilty for taking it, but told herself she would return it later. If she was going to convince her father that Edwin was a bad man, she needed physical evidence.

Maisie returned to the house to find Guvvy in hysterics. "You were gone for over four hours!" Guvvy said. "I was moments away from calling the police!" Her voice came out as a sob.

"I'm sorry I worried you," Maisie said.

"It's not safe for young girls out there," Guvvy said. "If you can't be trusted to come back within a reasonable amount of time, perhaps you shouldn't be trusted to go out alone."

It's not safe for young girls in here, either, Maisie thought, *what with you people trying to marry them to murderers and all.* But she only said, "I'm truly sorry,

Guvvy. I lost track of time, and it won't happen again. Is Papa home from work?"

"He's in his study. No doubt worrying about you."

"Well, then I'll stop in and let him know I'm all right." She marched down the hall and knocked on the door of the study.

"Yes?" Papa's voice called.

"Papa, it's me." She opened the door without waiting for his permission.

"Where in blue blazes have you been, girl?" Papa asked. "Harper was so upset I had to pour her a glass of brandy."

Maisie closed the door behind her. "I'm sorry for worrying everybody, but I need to talk to you about something important." She turned around so she could fish the newspaper out of her petticoat.

Papa sighed like nothing she had to tell him could possibly be important. "Well, be quick about it. I have work to do."

"Yes, sir," Maisie said, trying to hide her irritation. "I have reason to believe that Edwin may not be representing himself honestly," she said. She handed him the newspaper and pointed to the story.

She stood silently while he read.

Papa looked up and tossed the paper aside. "You did read here where it says he was cleared of all charges of wrongdoing?"

190

Maisie picked up the paper. It was the only evidence she had, and she was going to hang on to it. "I did," she said. "But doesn't it seem a little suspicious that he secured a large dowry from his first bride's father and then she died under mysterious circumstances shortly after the wedding? And now he's secured a large dowry from you—"

"Maisie, I will not tolerate such groundless speculation! If the medical examiner ruled that young woman's death an accident, then it was an accident. The medical examiner knows much more about such things than you or I do." Papa's face was a mask of anger. "Furthermore, I have spent many hours in the company of young Mr. Breedlove, and I have judged him to be a fine fellow. Harper!" Papa yelled. "Could you come here for a moment, please?"

Almost immediately, Guvvy appeared in the doorway.

"Harper, my daughter is exhibiting extraordinarily poor judgment today," Papa said. "I think she should be locked in her room for a few hours until she can think more clearly."

"Yes, sir," Guvvy said. With surprising strength, she grabbed Maisie's arm. "Come along now, Maisie," she said.

As Guvvy led her up the stairs, she said, "Now you've gone and made your papa angry. If I were you,

I'd spend some time today thinking about why it's a bad idea to squander this opportunity your papa has given you. Any other girl would be grateful."

Maisie didn't want to cry because she didn't want to seem weak, but tears of fear and anger burned in her eyes. "But you don't understand. I'm afraid."

Guvvy looked at her with something like kindness. "Dear, it's normal for girls to feel afraid of marriage. But you get used to it." They had arrived at Maisie's bedroom. "Now, go to your room and take some time to think." Guvvy took Maisie's hand and squeezed it.

Maisie cried out in pain.

Guvvy looked down at the long scratch marks. "What have you done to your hand?"

Maisie racked her brain for a plausible story. "Oh, at the park, there was a stray cat, and I . . . I tried to help it, and it scratched me."

Guvvy shook her head. "Yet more poor judgment from you today. I'll clean the wound when I come back to let you out."

Once Maisie was in her room, Guvvy closed the door. Maisie heard the lock click from the outside.

The only possible way out was the window, but she was on the second story and it was a straight drop down with no shrubbery to break her fall. Maisie's heart pounded in her chest. There was no way out. She was trapped. She was doomed.

CHAPTER 8

They hadn't broken her, but if she stood a chance of any kind, she had to appear obedient. For the past week, she hadn't ventured out any farther than the front yard. She was an attentive student in Guvvy's "classes," in what passed for an education for girls: rules of etiquette, memorization of sappy poems, china painting, needlework. Boys in this era went to school and learned normal academic subjects like math and science and history. But girls were "educated" to be qualified for only one profession: wives and mothers, and sooner rather than later. In her real life, Maisie had often complained about the difficulty of her high school classes, but now she could see the value of some of that hard work. At least she had been allowed to use her brain.

Today would be Maisie's most challenging day yet.

Edwin and Violet were coming to tea, and Guvvy was in a tizzy of excitement. "I had Annie press your tea gown," Guvvy said, holding out a light green dress with puffy sleeves.

There were special dresses you had to wear to drink tea? Maisie never failed to be amazed by this era's fussy attention to detail. *Were there,* she wondered, *other dresses that were appropriate only for the drinking of other beverages? "Oh dear, I'm terribly thirsty, but before I drink, I must change into my glass-of-water gown."* But all Maisie said aloud was, "That's nice."

It was always important for a young lady to look her best when drinking tea with a murderer. With *her* murderer, potentially.

Maisie hoped she would be able to control herself and sit in the living room politely with Edwin and Violet and Papa. She hoped her teacup wouldn't shake as she lifted it to her lips.

When there was the inevitable knock on the front door, Maisie felt her stomach contract in fear. Annie opened the door for Edwin and Violet. Edwin was decked out in a light gray cutaway suit and matching hat, which he gave to Annie to hang up. And Violet was wearing a periwinkle blue dress cut similarly to Maisie's—a tea gown, presumably. Violet was all smiles, very much the Violet whom Maisie had so recently called her friend.

"Maisie!" Violet squealed, then embraced her and kissed her cheek.

"My dearest," Edwin said. He took Maisie's hand and kissed it. His mustache scraped the scabs that had formed where Violet had scratched her.

The tea trolley Annie brought out was groaning with sandwiches and little cakes and tarts and cookies. Edwin loaded his plate and gobbled the dainty treats; Violet took only one small sandwich and cake and nibbled them delicately. Maisie felt too upset to eat; the best she could do was to sip her tea and try to keep her hands steady.

"Lovely weather we're having this spring," Violet said, smiling sweetly. "I do so enjoy the flowers this time of year."

"Well, naturally you would," Papa said, smiling back at her, "being named after a flower yourself!"

Everyone laughed much harder than Maisie thought was necessary, but she did muster a small smile in the hope of keeping up a proper appearance.

"Maisie, wouldn't it be lovely to have a garden party wedding?" Violet said, her eyes twinkling deceptively.

"Mm," Maisie said, trying to force herself to sound pleasant. "Guvvy suggested the wedding should be on my birthday."

Violet clapped her hands. "Now, that would be delightful! What do you think, Edwin? Would you like to have a birthday wedding party?"

"That sounds very jolly," Edwin said. His smile, Maisie thought, looked menacing. "Of course I'll be happy with a wedding any place, as long as my bride is there waiting for me."

Maisie felt a chill run through her. She hoped she hadn't visibly shivered.

"Such devotion!" Violet sighed. "Sometimes I think my brother is even more of a romantic than I am."

"It is so uplifting," Papa said, "to see two happy young people starting on life's journey together."

But I'm not happy, Maisie thought. *You know I'm not happy.*

Violet and Edwin were all smiles and pleasantries for the rest of the afternoon. Papa and Guvvy laughed at Edwin's forced jokes and Violet giggled on cue. *They really were expert liars*, Maisie thought. When the ordeal was finally over, Edwin, in the guise of kissing Maisie's cheek, whispered in her ear. "That was a much better performance than last time. Such behavior will be rewarded. Or at least, not punished."

Once the door shut behind them, Maisie said, "I think I'm going to lie down."

"Of course," Papa said. "That was a great deal of excitement, wasn't it? No wonder you need a rest."

Maisie had no intention of lying down. She needed to be away from those people. She needed time to plan. But to plan what? From its hiding place under the mattress, she took out the newspaper with the story about Edwin and studied it, hoping that reading between the lines about the horror of what happened to his first wife might cause some desperate spark of an idea to ignite in her brain.

She had nothing. She threw the newspaper across the room.

When she went to pick it up so she could hide it under the mattress again, an ad she hadn't noticed before caught her eye.

Are you being beset by dark forces? Are you lonely and longing for love? Do you wish to increase your good fortune or to speak with a departed loved one? Madam Pamplova, spirit medium, can use her gifts to travel to the past, future, and distant spiritual planes to guide you to a better tomorrow.

Maisie recognized Madam Pamplova's address as one of the side streets downtown. She knew that chances were that the "spirit medium" was probably a fraud whose only gift was separating gullible people from their money. Plus, the newspaper in which the madam's ad appeared was three years old. Maisie had no way of knowing if she was even still in business.

However, she was running out of options. Maybe a so-called "spirit medium" was worth a shot. Maisie had gotten here through unexplainable means; maybe she needed to use those means to get back, too.

After over two weeks of good behavior, Maisie was able to convince Guvvy that it was safe for her to go meet Violet downtown to shop for new spring hats at the milliner's.

But Maisie wasn't meeting Violet, and she wasn't going to the milliner's. She was going to see if Madam Pamplova was still in business. She turned down the side street listed in the ad and came to a tiny storefront. On the window was a small pasteboard sign hand-printed with the words *Madam Pamplova Spiritualist Clairvoyant Mesmerist.*

Maisie wasn't sure if she should knock or just go inside like it was a regular business. She tried the door-knob, and when it turned, she walked in. The room was small and draped in sheer curtains and crimson velvet. A low sofa covered in silk and satin throw pillows was arranged in front of a table laid out with a crystal ball on an ornate pewter stand and a stack of what Maisie recognized as tarot cards. *This must be the place,* she thought. But where was Madam Pamplova?

Her question was soon answered. The red velvet

curtains parted, and a woman emerged from between them. She was not what Maisie had imagined at all. She was younger, for one thing. Maybe it was the title "Madam," but Maisie had imagined an elderly woman. The woman standing before her, though, was perhaps in her early forties—around the same age as Maisie's mom. This fact reminded Maisie that she missed her mom terribly.

Madam Pamplova was also not decked out in the kind of garb fortune-tellers wore in old movies. She was pretty in an unadorned way, and wore a plain black, high-collared dress with black drop earrings and beads that Maisie recognized as Victorian mourning jewelry. Had Madam Pamplova lost someone close to her? And if so, was this the reason she had been drawn to spiritualism? She knew that one of the most frequent claims of spiritualists was that they had the ability to communicate with the dead.

"Welcome," Madam Pamplova said. She looked intently at Maisie for a long, awkward moment. "I see you are troubled."

"Yes," Maisie said, though she figured Madam probably said the same thing to everyone who walked through the door. "Yes, I am."

"I feel that if I gaze in the crystal, I will gain clarity about what ails you," Madam said. "What is your name, dear?"

"Maisie," she said, overcoming the temptation to say, *You're the psychic. You tell me.*

"I very much want to help you, Maisie. A crystal reading is one dollar."

Maisie peeled off a dollar from the bills Papa had doled out to her for hat shopping.

"Excellent," Madam said. "Let us sit down together." She gestured for Maisie to settle on the pillow-piled couch, then pulled up a high-backed chair so she was leaning over the crystal ball. She closed her eyes for a long time, which didn't seem conducive to gazing, but then opened them and focused hard on the clear orb. "Hmm," she said. "Hmmmm."

So far Maisie wasn't impressed with the schtick, which seemed well rehearsed but inauthentic.

Madam looked up at Maisie. "You are not of this time," she said.

"Wait—what?" Maisie said, so shocked she forgot to speak Victorian-ese.

"You are not of this time," Madam repeated. "You have traveled here from a future century."

"Yes," Maisie said. She felt amazement but also gratitude. For the first time since she had arrived here, she felt understood. "Yes, I have. Though, to be honest, I don't even know how I got here."

"That." Madam pointed at the chatelaine pinned to Maisie's dress.

"Yes." Maisie touched the chatelaine. "I know it's what brought me here. I just don't know how it brought me here."

"It is a cursed object," Madam Pamplova said. She stared at the piece of jewelry for a moment. "There is someone here who menaces you, yes?"

Maisie nodded vigorously. "The man my father wants me to marry. Not my real father, but my father in this place. I know if I marry this man, he'll kill me."

Madam Pamplova nodded gravely. "This man, the one who menaces you. You must destroy the cursed object in front of him. How you destroy it is up to you, but you must destroy it completely."

The idea seemed crazy, but hadn't everything seemed crazy since she had entered this dream that wasn't really a dream? "I'll do it," Maisie said. "Thank you. Thank you for being the only person here who has wanted to help me, even if I did have to pay you a dollar."

Madam Pamplova shrugged. "I would have helped for free if you had had no money. I do what I can, especially for women."

"It's good to know somebody does," Maisie said. "I don't know how you stand it here. Whenever I've tried to explain things to anyone, they act like I'm stupid or lying or both. But nobody questions what men say, even men who are obviously demented and dangerous."

"There is truth in that," Madam Pamplova said. "Tell me. In the future, is it better . . . for our sex?"

It wasn't a hard question to answer. Modern life for girls and women had many flaws, but still, it was a massive improvement over the Victorian era. "Yes," Maisie said. "Much better."

CHAPTER 9

It was a beautiful spring day, and Edwin and Violet had come by saying they were going downtown for an ice cream soda and asked Maisie to join them. It was strange to ask someone out for ice cream when you were planning to murder them, but Maisie supposed it was all about keeping up the appearance of being a happily engaged couple. People would see them at the ice cream parlor and later, when Maisie was dead, they could comment on how happy Maisie and Edwin had seemed together. And so, strange as it was, Maisie was walking to town with her murderers. Her enjoyment of the beauty of the blooming dogwoods and redbuds was a little hampered by her knowledge that she was in the presence of evil.

The chatelaine was pinned to her dress. She had to

destroy it in Edwin's presence, but how to destroy it? Was throwing it under a passing carriage so that it was crushed enough to do the job, or did she need to find a method that would more totally obliterate it?

"You're lost in thought today, aren't you, my pet?" Edwin said, spitting out *my pet* like an insult.

"I just didn't sleep well last night. I'm sorry," Maisie said, though she had actually slept better than she had in several nights. Her meeting with Madam Pamplova had given her a small piece of hope.

"A lady should always look and act well rested even when she isn't," Violet said. "Smile. Pretend that you're enjoying yourself."

Maisie became even more certain that they were creating an alibi by parading her around town like this and telling her to act happy, but to ensure her safety for the time being, she pasted a smile on her face.

As they approached the soda fountain, Maisie caught sight of another business that ignited an idea. This was it, she decided.

"Could we stop at the blacksmith's shop before we get ice cream?" Maisie asked. "I need to buy some nails to hang pictures in my room."

"Isn't that the kind of errand you can send your maid on?" Edwin asked, sounding irritable.

"Well, normally it would be, but you see, Annie was being courted by the blacksmith for several months, then it ended badly," Maisie lied, she thought rather convincingly. "I like to spare her the embarrassment of having to speak with him."

"You're too kind, Maisie," Violet said. They followed her into the blacksmith's shop.

The blacksmith was a large, muscular, bearded man. "May I help you folks?" he asked. For such a massive man, he was surprisingly soft-spoken.

"I've come to buy some nails," Maisie said, "but first I have a strange question."

The blacksmith had a pleasant smile. Edwin smiled only with his mouth, but the blacksmith smiled with his eyes as well. "I'll bet it's not the strangest one I ever heard. Ask me."

"Could you take us to see your forge?" Maisie said. She was suddenly so nervous that her voice was shaking.

He shrugged. "I don't see why not. It's right this way."

"What are you doing?" Edwin muttered under his breath.

"Indulging my curiosity," Maisie said. "I'm fascinated by fire. Besides, you want me to look happy, don't you?"

The forge had a metal cover shaped like the roof of a house and a pipe that served as a sort of chimney. Under the cover, orange flames burned over glowing coals. "So that fire is hot enough to melt metal?" Maisie asked.

"Yes, at its hottest point it is, Miss." The blacksmith seemed puzzled but was still good-natured.

"And where would the hottest point be?" Maisie asked.

"You see the part right at the lip of the firepot where it looks blue?" the blacksmith said.

"Yes, sir," Maisie said.

"That's the hottest point."

"Thank you," Maisie said.

In what seemed like one swift motion, Maisie unpinned the chatelaine from her dress and threw it into the hottest part of the forge. She watched it as it became engulfed in flames, glowed blue, then melted.

From behind her, Maisie heard screaming.

She turned around to see Edwin, his skin sweating, then reddening, then charring. Clouds of smoke were rising from his clothes. He screamed like a tortured soul, then fell to the ground, writhing, as orange and blue flames rose seemingly from nowhere and lapped at his clothes and body.

"Edwin!" Violet screamed and threw herself on her brother in an attempt to snuff out the flames. But then the hem of her dress was on fire, too, and her screams joined his.

The blacksmith came running with a bucket of

water while Maisie stood by watching the growing blaze, fascinated. But then the flames blurred into an indistinct orange, then blue, and finally faded to black.

Maisie was gone.

Maisie's eyes opened. She didn't see the curtains and canopy, but she didn't see her real room, either. She didn't know where she was.

"Are you awake?" her mom asked. She said it like Maisie being awake was not an everyday thing, but instead a momentous occasion. "Oh thank God, you're awake!"

When Maisie tried to speak, her voice came out as a croak. Her mom poured some water from a plastic pitcher into a plastic cup with a straw and offered it to her. Maisie drank gratefully. She was so thirsty. But she wasn't just grateful for the water. She was grateful to finally see her mom again.

"You're in the hospital, sweetie," Mom said. "You've been unconscious for three days, and none of the doctors have been able to figure out why."

Maisie looked down to see that she was indeed in a narrow hospital bed, wearing an ugly hospital gown. An IV was attached to her arm. "Mom," she asked, her scratchy voice sounding like someone else's. "When you brought me here, was I wearing any jewelry?"

"Okay, so that's not the first the question I thought you'd ask," Mom said. "But let's see . . . there's a plastic bag over here with everything you were wearing when I brought you in." She got up and riffled through the white plastic bag, pulling out Maisie's pajama top and bottoms and a pair of socks, then said, "Hmm . . . that's strange."

"What?" Maisie said.

"Well, I seem to remember you had on some kind of brooch, which I thought was weird since you were in your pajamas, but all I found in the bag was . . . this." She held out a twisted, melted-looking lump of silver.

"Good," Maisie said, exhaling in relief. "Good." She was glad the chatelaine was no longer recognizable, glad to be back in the time where she now knew she belonged.

"We need to call your dad," Mom said. "He'll be so excited that you're awake."

On the way home from the hospital, Maisie said, "Mom, can we stop by the lake for a minute?"

"I don't know," Mom said. "You're still not that

strong. I'd rather get you all settled and comfy at home."

"Please, Mom. It'll just take a minute. There's something I really need to do."

"Well, okay," Mom said, though she was using her reluctant voice. She pulled over into the parking lot.

"Mom, can you hand me that plastic bag with my things in it?"

"All right, but I don't understand—"

"It's okay. I just need to grab something." She dug through the bag and pulled out the twisted lump that had been the chatelaine. "I'll be right back, okay?"

"Let me walk with you," Mom said.

"Okay."

Maisie was thankful for her mom's support. Her legs were a little wobbly as she walked up to the edge of the water. She mustered all the strength she had and threw the lump of metal as far out into the lake as she could. She heard the splash and imagined it sinking down to the bottom where no one would ever find it again.

Now she was ready to go home.

EPILOGUE

The woman in the black velvet Victorian dress set the glass cases out on the folding tables. The flea market's doors would open in half an hour, so she was a little more rushed than she liked to be. Fortunately, most of the jewelry was already in the glass cases; it just needed to be rearranged from where it had shifted during travel. She liked everything to be arranged just so, such that the beams of sunlight shining through the narrow window would hit the stones and make them sparkle.

And then there was the one new piece she had to put out on display. Well, none of her pieces were *new* really, but some of them were new to her collection. This one was special. It had been sold a while back, but as her pieces often did after they had served their purposes for their owners, it had found its way back to her.

In an empty glass case, the woman spread out a beautiful piece of deep purple velvet. Right in the center of the cloth, where the light would hit it just right, she placed the chatelaine. It was perfect. The woman looked up to see a teenaged girl dressed all in black approaching her booth, and she turned on her most-welcoming smile.

ABOUT THE AUTHOR

Elley Cooper writes fiction for young adults and adults. She has always loved horror and is grateful whenever she can spend time in a dark and twisted universe. Elley lives in Tennessee with her family and many spoiled pets and can often be found writing books with Kevin Anderson & Associates.